TOUCH OF THE CLOWN

Glen Huser

TOUCH
OF THE
CLOWN

A Groundwood Book

DOUGLAS & McINTYRE

TORONTO VANCOUVER BUFFALO

YA
HUS

My appreciation to my family and friends who read the first drafts of
Touch of the Clown and offered many helpful comments.
A special thanks to my editor, Shelley Tanaka, for her insightful
suggestions throughout the revision process.

Copyright © 1999 by Glen Huser

Groundwood Books / Douglas & McIntyre Ltd.
585 Bloor Street West, Toronto, Ontario M6G 1K5

Distributed in the USA by Publishers Group West
1700 Fourth Street, Berkeley, CA 94710

We acknowledge the financial support of the Canada Council for the Arts,
the Ontario Arts Council and the Government of Canada through the Book
Publishing Industry Development Program for our publishing activities.

Library of Congress Data is available

Canadian Cataloguing in Publication Data
Huser, Glen, 1943-
Touch of the clown
A Groundwood book.
ISBN 0-88899-343-9 (bound) ISBN 0-88899-357-9 (pbk.)
I. Title.
PS8565.U823T68 1999   jC813'.54   C98-932840-6
PZ7.H87To 1999

Cover illustration: Janet Wilson
Design: Michael Solomon
Printed and bound in Canada

For Ian
— and in memory of David

CHAPTER ONE

Summer holidays are the worst times. I know they're supposed to be great, and I remember a long time ago when I finished grade one and we went to Alberta Beach for the summer and it was great, but that was the last time, that summer when Mama was still alive and Olivia de Havilland was waiting to be born.

Mama and I made dill-pickle sandwiches and filled big glass sealers with lemonade and ice. We took our beach towels and comic books and word-search puzzles and a little radio and sunscreen down to the beach and stayed there sometimes all day, just loafing and laughing and wading in the water or wandering out on the long pier to let the breeze blow on us and cool us off.

Mama had a big picture of Jimmy Dean on her towel, the one that her girlfriend Marilyn Marsden sent her from L.A.

"I sure do like to cozy up to Jimmy on a hot summer day," Mama would laugh. "Marilyn and I were just crazy about him when we were teenagers. Rub my legs with oil again, will you, honey? And I'll do your back." My towel had Care Bears on it, but it hadn't come from L.A., just from Woolco.

Mama would lie on her back and let her fingers make little circles on her tummy. "If anyone asks you, you just tell them that I swallowed a beach ball," she would whoop with laughter, showing all of her big, crooked teeth.

You might wonder where my dad and Grandma Kobleimer were while we were at the beach all day. Once in awhile they would wander down for maybe twenty minutes before Daddy would say he could feel himself breaking out in a heat rash and Grandma would say something about only mad dogs and Englishmen going out in the noonday sun. Then they'd head back to the cottage, close the living-room drapes and search for movies on the TV.

That was seven years ago when I was six.

That good summer.

I would lie on the beach under the sun and even then I could do a word search faster than Mama.

"You whiz-kid," she would say. "You little bright button. Where'd you find that big long word? I've been looking for fifteen minutes."

We'd finish our word searches and read our comics, and then we'd have a tell-me time.

"Tell me how you met Daddy," I might say, even though I knew the story already.

"Well," Mama would say, holding the word in her mouth like you would a peppermint candy, "we were both working in a little old theater downtown."

"You were the popcorn lady."

"I was the popcorn lady and your daddy was the ticket-taker and sometimes an usher. When there weren't many people in the audience and it was the final show, we'd slip into the back row and watch the last feature, and one time he took my hand in his. The show was *The Wizard of Oz* on a rerun, I think."

Or I might say, "Tell me how I got my name."

"Well," again rolling the word around in her mouth, "your daddy and I made a deal. He would get to name any girls we would have, and I would get to name the boys. When you came along he said, 'I'm going to name this little one Barbara Stanwyck.' You see, Barbara Stanwyck was always his favorite actress. He used to drag me miles to see a Barbara Stanwyck movie, or we'd stay up half the night if one was coming on the Late Late Show. So that's how you got your name. Barbara Stanwyck Kobleimer. Now, if this beach ball turns out to be a boy, I'm going to name him James Dean, and we'll call him Jimmy, of course."

Sometimes I look at Livvy and think what it would have been like if she had been a little boy with no health problems, and Mama had lived. Jimmy Dean and Mama and I would go to the beach and build sand castles and walk out on the long pier where you can look down and the water is so clear you can see the wave patterns in the sand and the water weeds doing their slow, slow dance. And then we would lie on our beach towels and do word searches. Words with double letters are easy to find—forwards, backwards, or going on a slant. Words like HAPPINESS. You just look for any two p's together and figure it out from there. I would show Jimmy Dean how to do it.

Today it is extra hot, and with the door closed and the blinds down so there won't be any glare on the TV, the air inside is heavy and sticky. Daddy's face is covered with little beads of sweat, which he clears away every few minutes with a hand towel. Grandma doesn't sweat as much, maybe because she covers the parts of her that show with powder. But I know the heat is getting to her, too. She has a small electric fan on top of her ornament shelf, with its airstream aimed at her face. It blows along the rows of little bluish curls on her head.

"I wish we could go and stay at the lake for awhile this summer," I say, kind of casual, setting down their lunch trays. The macaroni and cheese is fresh and the toast isn't burnt, and there's little juice glasses with ice in them, in case they want their sherry over ice. I've been planning this all morning. "Maybe we could go to Alberta Beach and it wouldn't be so hot there and Livvy and I could go to the beach by the long pier. I know Livvy would like it."

Daddy has a forkful of macaroni halfway to his mouth but he puts it down with a clatter on the plate.

"Are you crazy?" he begins yelling. "You want to have Olivia at the beach, running every fifteen minutes to wash out her clothes in a public toilet? Is that your idea of fun? No, thank you, miss. We have a cross to bear but we'll bear it close to an automatic washing machine and a gas dryer, if you please."

"Look what you've done," Grandma hisses at me when Daddy's left the room and banged into the bathroom. I can hear him, over the water running, beginning to cry.

Livvy is hollering from downstairs, "Baaarbara, I need you," which means she's had an accident and needs to be changed.

"You make your daddy feel real bad that he can't take you any place for a holiday. You've made a grown man cry."

"Baaarbara."

"He'd be crying anyway by suppertime," I mutter. "He always cries after he's had a few glasses of sherry."

"What a thing to say." Grandma seems to shrink into her easy chair, as if she's getting ready to spring. "That man has made every sacrifice for his daughters and you have the unmitigated gall to throw into his face the small bit of solace he obtains from a drink to settle his nerves."

Grandma Kobleimer should work for the word-search people. I've never seen "unmitigated" or "solace" in any puzzle I've ever done. She could keep the word-search people busy for days.

"Baaarbara, I need you."

"I'm coming." I give Livvy an answering yell, heading for the basement stairs before Grandma can get her second wind.

Livvy has already got herself out of her clothes, which lie in a heap on the floor by her feet.

"You'd better get upstairs into a tub," I say, picking up the clothes to rinse in the laundry sink. "You can put on your shorts and your Batman T-shirt when you get out."

"Oh, goood-ee." Livvy does a little dance and claps her hands. I give her my you-don't-need-to-act-like-a-little-baby look. Livvy likes to act, but I guess you can't blame her. If I had her problem, I think I'd pretend I was someone else, too.

I run hot water onto the clothes in the tub and watch the soiled water rise up before pulling the plug, rinsing them again and adding them to the pile of clothes already waiting to become a full load in the washing machine.

Livvy has changed by the time I get back upstairs, and she lies on the rug, devouring her bowl of macaroni and cheese. Sometimes I think that if I were Livvy I would never eat anything and then the problem would just go away, but Livvy has a different outlook on things. She'd be quite happy pushing something in her mouth twenty-four hours a day.

Daddy is back from the bathroom, but his face is still wet from tears, and he has poured the juice glass full of sherry. "Where's the justice?" He dabs at the tears and sweat with the hand towel. "To lose her mother, and then lose a kidney. How does she stand a chance? We couldn't go on a holiday even if we had the money."

"There is no justice," Grandma nods over her own juice glass half filled with sherry. "No justice in the world. But I tell you, son, what you have to put up with, there'll be a crown of stars waiting in heaven for you. How many men would do what you do? Stay home..."

But at that moment the MGM lion roars on the TV and both of them pause, suddenly speechless as the title of a movie rolls across a Technicolor sky. Even Livvy stops for a moment, her spoonful of macaroni hovering in midair with a small trail of cheese sauce spilling onto the living-room rug.

"I'm going out for awhile," I announce. This is the safest time to make a getaway, just as a new movie is sucking them in.

Livvy takes advantage of her already open mouth to begin a howl of protest, but I quickly say, "You come, too, Livvy. Hurry and finish your macaroni."

CHAPTER TWO

We have always lived in Grandma Kobleimer's house, an old house like the others on the street. It is a sad part of town where tired, homeless people sometimes lie down in the crabgrass along the back alleys or even on the boulevard, and it is sometimes hard to tell if they are sleeping or dead. Daddy says not to go near any people who are lying down outside and to run away fast if any strange person tries to come up to us. Most of the kids in my neighborhood can run fast when they need to. I've been trying to get Livvy to practice running but it's not her favorite thing to do.

"You want to go to the playground?" I ask her now as she hops from foot to foot, not sure about which direction to take.

"The one with the curly slide?"

"Sure," I say. If you've seen one playground, you've seen them all. Fenceposts and rubber tires and metal pipes. A curly slide or a straight slide. Bad words written wherever there's space enough to write something. "But if there's a bunch of kids there, we're not going."

"I'm not scared of kids." Livvy begins skipping in circles.

"Well, I am."

There's no playground really close to where we live. You need to walk a few blocks to get to any of them. There are girls out already on some of the corners, in hot pants and high heels. The trick is to get Livvy past them without her stopping to chat. It means crossing the road a lot.

Actually, before you start along any block, you look to see if there are people staggering or any tough kids on the watch for someone to be mean to. And whether or not there are girls on the corner.

Livvy hasn't figured this out yet. She doesn't know what can happen. I've been beaten up twice. The first time was when I was in grade three and I was going to the store to get Froot Loops and milk. Three junior-high girls stopped me and said, "Hey, kid, got any spare change?" I didn't even know what spare change meant, and of course my mouth seized up and just a funny little croaking noise came out. My fist clamped tighter around the five dollars Grandma had given me along with a big lecture about how I wasn't to lose any of the money that was left.

"Whatcha got in your hand, kid?" One of the girls could see my knuckles were turning white hanging onto something, so two of them held me and the third one pried my fingers open.

"Now that's not nice," the biggest one laughed. "Didn't your momma tell you about sharing? I guess we're just gonna have to learn you a lesson."

Of course, by that time, I was howling my head off.

"Shut up, or we'll give you something to cry about," said the girl who had a tattoo of a skull and a snake on her arm. Before they ran off with the five dollars, this one knocked me down onto the sidewalk and kicked my legs. I lay there for a long time crying before I got up, scraped bits of gravel off my knees and hands, and limped home.

Daddy and Grandma were furious and they did a lot of yelling about what was the world coming to, and where were the police when you needed them, but they never phoned in a complaint. Neither of them really liked to have anything to do with the police.

After that, I knew you had to be suspicious of just about everyone who's bigger than you when you're on the sidewalk, except for old ladies with white hair.

But last year, the second time I got beaten up, I didn't have a chance. Two boys came bombing out of the pool hall just as I was going by with a bagful of videos to return to the video store. They grabbed the videos, and one twisted my arm really hard and said to give him any money I had. It turned out I only had twenty-seven cents in my pocket, and when they saw how it was such a little bit, the one twisted my arm even harder until I thought it would crack.

"Aw, let her be," said the guy with my bag of videos. "She's just a kid." He even smiled at me, big chipped teeth showing through a faceful of pimples.

The other one just kind of snarled, like a dog, and grabbed me by my cheek and pinched really hard before letting me go. By that time I'd found my voice and was screaming as loud as I could. They ran off. My arm hurt so bad I thought I was going to die, and I sat down on a bus-stop bench and cried until it felt a little bit better.

Then I was afraid to go home because of the videos. There were two new releases and four from the three-day rental shelves.

Daddy and Grandma were already in a bad mood when I finally straggled in. Livvy had had a major accident while I was out and they'd had to clean her up. This time they did call the police, but it didn't help anything, and we had to pay $215.00 to the video store, which took all of our grocery money for one month.

"I don't know why you can't be trusted to go four blocks by yourself," Daddy yelled at me, as if it were my fault I got mugged.

So today Livvy and I cross the street four times just to be on the safe side before we get to the park with the curly slide.

Livvy is good for about two hours at the play-ground if she doesn't have an accident. I push her on the swings a bit and say "hey," and wave when she hollers, "Baarbra, look at me!" as she works her way along monkey bars or climbs up into the little wooden tower. But mostly I sit at the picnic table with my survival bag, the straw beach bag Mama used to take with us to Alberta Beach. Some of the straw is coming loose, but I glue the pieces back with my white school glue.

In the bag I have a change of clothing for Livvy, my word-search magazine, a library book, and a scribbler that's good for playing X's and O's with Livvy or for making notes to myself, a box of crayons and an old scrapbook from grade five, which Livvy uses when she feels like making pictures. There are a few other things, too, which I carry for good luck: a little pink glass bottle that once held some of Mama's perfume, a letter from Marilyn Marsden from L.A. that says, "I hope sometime you can come and visit me. Your mama always wanted to come, and now that she isn't with us, you need to come for her." I know the letter by heart. This is only part of it.

My library book today is called *Looking at the Moon*. It is about a big family at a beach, and they live in a cottage that has a whole bunch of rooms, and there's a boathouse and a pier. Norah, the girl in the story, isn't really part of the family. She's been sent from England to get away from the war. When you read the book you're supposed to be thinking about Norah and how she's falling in love and it's not working out very well, but I keep thinking about the beach and the trees alongside it, and the clear water, and the sounds of children shouting, and seagulls dipping and diving like kites.

In this family, a cook makes the meals and I imagine things like oatmeal porridge and bacon and eggs and pancakes. I want to be Norah with her sore heart and her worries about the war and her family back in England.

"Baarbraaa—look what I found." Livvy is dancing over from the playground equipment. She's holding a rubber ball in her hand. It is a faded grayish-green covered with a pattern of stars.

"Look, starshine," she says. At one time the stars must have been covered with glitter paint. Most of the glitter has worn off, but here and there a little fleck catches the sunlight.

"Play ball with me," Livvy begs, dancing around, throwing the ball up in the air, trying to catch it, chasing it across the grass and the gravel.

"Okay," I say, "but we've got to go soon." A cluster of teenagers moving across the field toward the playground makes me decide to leave even sooner. I throw the word search and *Looking at the Moon* into the survival bag. "We can play catch on the way home."

Which isn't such a great idea because Livvy can never catch the ball and ends up spending all of her time chasing it along the sidewalk and sometimes even into the street as I scream at her to look out for cars in my fiercest imitation of Grandma Kobleimer.

Livvy is having a great afternoon. Somehow the ball with its sad little glittery stars has made her feel like a winner. She hops and skips as she goes along, and claps her hands, and sings a song that she learned at school about a dog named Bingo.

"I'm gonna call this ball Bingo," she informs me. "Bingo is my ball-o."

There are two girls in high heels at the next corner, so I hiss at her, "Cross here, Livvy."

And then it happens. She throws the ball ahead of her so that it goes bouncing into the street, and before I can yell at her, she is chasing it down the middle of the road. A car swerves, startling her so that she darts into the oncoming lane and a man on a bicycle runs right into her.

Have you ever noticed how, when something truly terrible happens, the world stops for a few seconds? Nothing seems to move. I can hear, faintly, the sound of a ghetto blaster from an open upstairs window across the street. Somewhere a dog barks. The car that swerved to avoid Livvy moves on. I am like a statue, pure stone.

Just a couple of seconds and then Livvy's cry shatters the air and sets everything in motion. Another oncoming car screeches as it stops and then swings around the tangled pile of Livvy and the man on the bicycle. My feet move at a run.

CHAPTER THREE

By the time I get there, Livvy has pulled herself away from the man and the bicycle. She is sitting on the pavement holding her knee, screaming nonstop. There is blood all down one leg, and blood on her hands, and more blood starting to ooze from a gash in her forehead.

The man untangles himself from the bicycle. He is bleeding, too, but just above one hand, and he quickly unties his neckerchief and wraps it around his forearm.

I am there now, with my arm around Livvy's shoulders, my hands brushing at her cheeks, trying to smooth away the tears, wipe off the blood. "It's okay, honey-pie," I croon. "It's okay." And I rock her a bit.

The man is on his feet now and he picks up his bicycle and lays it on the grass between the sidewalk and the curb.

"Let's get her off the street," he says, all the time making funny rag-doll shaking movements with his arms and legs, tilting his head toward one shoulder and then the other, and moving his jaw like he's checking to see if anything is broken.

"Gee, I'm sorry," he says, crouching down next to Livvy. "I didn't have time to get out of your way. Are you okay? Let's see if you can get up." He has a soft, gentle voice, and he smiles at me, just a quick smile filled with white teeth. It's then I notice he is dressed differently from most men we see in this part of town. He has on a T-shirt the color of egg yolk, blue suspenders, faded red jeans and green running shoes the color of limes.

Livvy's mouth is open but no sound is coming out at the moment. Just a little rattle at the back of her throat.

"See if you can get her to move her arms and legs—just a bit to start with," the man says to me. "I've been bleeding so I'd better not handle her."

Livvy has found her voice again, a howl that can shatter windows.

"Sssh, baby-pie." I hug her closer and rock her a bit more. A car honks its horn as it goes by. "We've got to get off this street. Let's see if you can move your arms." I feel along her arms and get her to bend them. The blood is coming from a big scrape I can see. "Now let me help you up."

"I can't." Livvy has found her voice. "I'm dying," she screams.

"Try, sweetie-pie. Try for Barbara." I hold onto her, my arms wrapped around her chest, and gradually lift her.

"Owww." She softens her cry to a wail when she finds out her legs still work.

"Atta girl," says the man. "Just a few steps and we're off the road."

I end up carrying her, easing her onto the grass. Livvy has stopped crying for a minute, suddenly intrigued by the man of many colors. And, by this time, one of the girls in high heels has hobbled over to us.

"You okay, honey?" she asks. Livvy is looking at the pattern of black lace butterflies flying up the girl's net stockings to her leather skirt. "I seen it. You shouldn't run out in the road no matter what or you could get killed." She smiles a big lipstick smile at Livvy. "You need some help or something?"

"No, I think she'll be okay," the man smiles.

"I think it's mainly scrapes and scratches. Are you close to home?"

"We're about six blocks away," I calculate.

Suddenly Livvy opens her mouth in a howl again, as if she's been hit by a bicycle for the second time. "Bingo," she screams. "I want Bingo."

"Bingo?" The man and the lady in high heels speak at the same time.

"Her ball," I say. "The ball she was chasing."

The man in the colored clothes places his hand overtop of his eyes and bobs his head up and down like a bird. He makes me think of someone who is acting. "Aha," he says. "I spy Bingo." Waiting for traffic to clear, he lopes across the road to a fence on the other side and plucks Bingo out of a clump of crabgrass.

"There. Ya see, honey?" The girl in the high heels lights a cigarette and squats awkwardly in her tight skirt, just in front of Livvy. "Ya got your ball back now. Ain't that lucky?" She plucks some tissues out of her purse and dabs at Livvy's forehead. "Ya got a little cut there but it ain't too bad. My old man give me worse." She winks at me.

He is back with the ball but he doesn't give it to Livvy right away. Instead, he tucks it under

28

his chin. Rummaging through a backpack attached to the bicycle seat, he pulls out three colored balls. Magically, he tosses the balls into the air, adds Bingo, and continues juggling, the neckerchief bandage a blue blur, all the time making funny faces at Livvy.

Both Livvy and I are speechless, and Livvy seems to have momentarily forgotten her wounds. "Well, will you look at that," the girl in high heels says in a whisper. But her friend at the corner is hollering, "C'mon, Melody," and she reaches into her purse, pulls out a loonie and presses it into Livvy's blood-stained hands. "You buy yourself a little treat, honey," she says. Sighing, she rises from her crouch, adjusts her skirt and heads back to the corner.

I can see Livvy thinks this day has turned into some kind of strange dream, and I'm beginning to think so, too. The juggler is throwing the balls higher and higher into the air, finally scooping the three colored ones into a kangaroo pocket in his T-shirt. Then he clasps Bingo in both hands and presents it to Livvy like one of the three wise men bringing a gift to the baby Jesus.

"Behold, Bingo," he says.

Livvy actually laughs, and then, remembering

herself, turns it into a prolonged moan.

"I live just down the street here. You come along with me and we'll get you washed up, and do you know—" he looks Livvy directly in the eye, "I have some Band-Aids that glow in the dark. I think you're going to need at least ten or eleven."

I remember all of the things I have ever been told about never going anywhere with a stranger. "We'd better get home," I say. I cannot believe this man in his rainbow clothes, juggling for Livvy even while his arm is bandaged, can be bad, but it is better to be safe.

He seems to be reading my mind. "We'll do a little front yard ministration," he says. "There's a place where we can sit down, and I'll nip up to my flat and get some water and bandages. Do you want me to call your folks from my phone?"

"Naw. It's okay." I don't want to tell him our phone was cut off when Daddy didn't pay the bill for three months.

"Before we go anywhere, though," he smiles his wide smile, "we need some names. You have before you Cosmo Farber." And he does a little bow. "My mangled companion," he makes a sad clown mouth and points to the bicycle, "is Mehitabel."

"My name is Olivia de Havilland Kobleimer," Livvy shouts. I watch Cosmo do a mock staggering back, as if the name has struck him.

"You're kidding me," he says.

"No kidding," I say. "She's Olivia de Havilland and I'm Barbara Stanwyck. My dad suffers from a bad case of old-movie illness."

"Hey, you're all right," Cosmo laughs. "You support the wounded Olivia de Havilland, and I'll tend Mehitabel."

"And I'll take Bingo." Livvy takes a few tentative, limping steps and makes a little song of moans and ows mixed in with a bit of "Bingo is my ball-o."

"Olivia de Havilland and Barbara Stanwyck." Cosmo shakes his head. He is carrying Mehitabel in front of him. One wheel is all twisted. "Here we are," he says. We stop in front of an old three-story house with a verandah and an outside stairway leading up to the second and third floors.

The yard is crowded with bushes and flowers, a bird bath and a patio table with a broken umbrella, half of its flowered vinyl stretched over spokes, the other half caved in as if something has tried to land on it.

Cosmo leans the wounded Mehitabel against the table. "You guys park yourselves here and I'll go and get some warm water and a washcloth and some Band-Aids. You be okay for a couple of minutes, Olivia?"

"Livvy?" I can see she is on the verge of tears again, now that she's had a chance to sit down and take an inventory of her injuries.

"Livvy." Cosmo tries out the name while he rummages for a key. "We'll get you all fixed up in just a jiffy—a little washeroo, some glow-in-the-dark Band-Aids. Would you like something to drink?"

"Oh, goodee," Livvy slips into her baby talk and claps her hands together, forgetting they are bruised and scraped. "Ow, ooo." Tears well in her eyes.

"Where do you want to sit, Livvy? The patio chair or the bench?" It is enough to divert her attention. I search in the survival bag and bring out the scrapbook and crayons. "Why don't you draw a picture of Bingo ball?"

"I want to draw a picture of Cosmo and Bingo and those other balls." She has her tongue between her teeth as she starts to color on a blank page. She is still creating the picture when

Cosmo returns carrying a tray with an ice-cream pail of warm water, a washcloth and a towel, and a smaller tray with drinks in tall glasses.

"Mmm. Yum-yum." Livvy abandons the picture when she sees the lemonade.

Cosmo has turned the scribbler toward him so he can see the drawing. "Wow." He makes big eyes at Olivia. "Maybe we should rename her Olivia da Vinci. Now let's take a look at these wounds."

He is very gentle, sponging off the dried blood. With the blood washed away, we can see the actual damage: the gash on Livvy's forehead, a scrape on one arm, scraped hands, and one knee skinned. It takes two glow-in-the-dark Band-Aids to cover the knee, one on her forehead, one on each hand and three on her scraped arm. Livvy seems to gather strength with each patch. She is enchanted with the Band-Aids, twisting her arm back and forth, admiring her knee.

We sit at the patio table. The sidewalk is beginning to be busy with people going home from work. They look at the three of us sipping tall glasses of lemonade, with little trickles of moisture running along the sides of the glasses.

A small, quiet picnic in the middle of rush hour.

"Hey, buddy," a bearded man lurches against the picket fence. "That lemon gin?"

"Not a chance," Cosmo laughs.

"You gotta cigarette, man?"

"Don't smoke."

"Well, this ain't my idea of a party." He grins and tips a greasy baseball cap to us before weaving off down the sidewalk.

"Par-tee," Livvy purrs. "I love parties."

"The patient is recovering," Cosmo whispers to me. "Now tell me about yourselves, Miss Barbara and Miss Olivia. I know you're on summer vacation, but what grade are you going into this fall?"

Livvy mugs a smile at him and holds up two fingers.

"She's going into grade two," I say, "and I'm going into grade eight." What else can I tell him? "We live with Dad and Grandma over on the street with the churches. We were just coming from the park." And then I make a bold move. "Are you an actor?" I ask.

"Actor, magician, dancer, juggler, clown," Cosmo laughs, "and sometimes a waiter."

"A waiter?"

"Yeah. Waiting for jobs." The afternoon sun makes his hair look like soft gold. It is short hair, thinning on top. "Sometimes waiting on tables."

"A clown!" Livvy shouts.

"Yes, Miss Olivia de Havilland Kobleimer. A clown. In fact, right now I'm doing clown workshops downtown. I'll be finishing this first one next week."

"A clown!"

"Yes. That is, when I'm not running down little kids on my bicycle."

His arms move a lot when he talks, and the bandage swoops and darts like a bird on his wrist. I can see there are bruises along his arms, and I think he must have been hurt more than we thought when he ran into Livvy.

"Now, tell me what you're going to be when you grow up," he says.

"I'm going to be a fireman," says Livvy through the long slurping sounds she is making at the end of her lemonade.

Usually when people ask me this, I say lifeguard. I can see myself at a big sandy public beach, sitting high up under the sun in a lifeguard chair, and down below me are kids splashing and building sandcastles, and people lying on the beach suntanning, some of them reading, some of them doing word searches. But now, when Cosmo asks me, I surprise myself.

"An actress," I say.

"Well, kid," Cosmo chuckles, "you got the right name for it."

An actress. Livvy is chattering away to Cosmo about the trip her grade one class took to the firehall last spring and, for a minute, I let what I've said soak into me. Is it something a person could actually put down as a career choice on those little personal inventory sheets our school counselor, Mr. Graydon, makes us fill out? Dentist. Gas-station attendant. Actress.

"You might like to get involved in the workshop that's starting in a couple of weeks. It's for kids fifteen and up, but it's not full and I could probably squeeze you in."

For no reason, I feel my face flushing.

"Seriously, think about it," Cosmo says.

The rush hour seems to be winding down. Fewer people on the sidewalk, mothers calling kids in to supper, traffic thinning.

"Maybe I should come home with you. In case your dad or your grandma have any questions about the accident," Cosmo proposes as I check to make sure everything is in place in the survival bag.

"We'll be okay. Thanks," I add.

Livvy is chasing Bingo around the yard. "Come here, you stupid ball!" she shrieks.

"Yes, I guess Miss Olivia de Havilland is going to live after all. But here, before you put your scribbler away, let me write my phone number down. If it's okay with your folks, maybe you and Livvy can pop over when I get home from work tomorrow—no, make that the day after tomorrow—and I'll give you a brochure on the clown workshop. Have to pick some up from the office. Any time after four."

"Sure," I say. "I'll check."

CHAPTER FOUR

I think about the clown workshop all the way home while Livvy sings her Bingo song. The more I think about it, the more I think it is something I want to do.

The school that Livvy and I go to offers a drama option in grade seven.

"I'll put you down for it," Mr. Graydon told me at the start of last year. Mr. Graydon has me come into his office often. He has an old sofa chair by his window, where you can look out and see the rooftops of buildings for blocks around.

"When I listened to you doing that reader's theater part in Mrs. Femeruk's class last year, I made a mental note to make sure you get into Ms. Billings' drama class this year."

I am always surprised at how much he knows about me. Mr. Graydon keeps a little bowl of pretzels on his desk. He likes to give visitors to the counselor's office a pretzel or two. In addition to the pretzels, he gives me compliments.

When he starts, I count the church spires. You can see four in the winter, but only two in September when the leaves are still on the trees.

"I understand you've read your way around the world," he tells me. "A book for each of twenty different countries. Mrs. Mattingley says you take out three or four books a week. Do you do anything else for recreation?"

"Watch movies," I say. "Daddy and Grandma like movies."

"What about you?"

"Sure," I say. "Who wouldn't?"

Another time he asks me about Livvy. "How's she doing at home? She's been having lots of accidents at school."

"She has...a few accidents at home, too." I feel my face going red.

"Of course it helps that you've been keeping a change of clothes in the nurse's office." Mr. Graydon passes me the pretzels. "Take a few," he says.

Livvy's problem is not one of my favorite subjects. Sometimes I wish she could have something clean and simple like scoliosis or acute sight loss. I've read books where girls had these diseases. They were handicaps that everyone

39

understood. Then I feel guilty. After all, there are times when Livvy can go for several days with no accidents at all, just as if she were a normal person. Just as if she'd never had one kidney removed, never had a bathroom problem.

The doctors can't seem to decide how to fix Livvy. They put her on special diets. They give Daddy bottles of pills for her to take and charts to keep. But Daddy loses track. I tried to make Livvy take the last bottle of medicine until it was finished. Livvy kept spitting the pills out, muttering, "Yuckee, yuckee." For awhile we had diapers for her to wear, but Livvy made such a fuss about putting them on that we quit trying.

Mr. Graydon watches me chew the pretzels.

"And how is she getting along? Livvy?"

"The kids tease her. Hold their noses. Call her names. Stinky. Livvy Le Pew."

"Who?"

"I don't know. Just kids."

Mr. Graydon sighs and shuts his eyes for a minute.

"Livvy uses the F-word on them," I add. "I've been telling her not to."

"Maybe she needs to."

I look at him sideways and notice he's not smiling.

"How about your dad? Has he been working lately?"

"He needs to stay home to look after Livvy," I tell him, "and he hasn't been well."

"Oh."

"He has bad nerves. They tried to fix them in the hospital."

Mr. Graydon looks at me. "The nerves?"

"He has medicine but it ran out."

"I see."

Sometimes when Mr. Graydon starts asking about things at home, I close off his voice. I read the posters on the wall behind him. Most of the posters have slogans. Things like "I will is more important than I.Q." Or I look out the window and count the houses that have black roofs, and then the green.

Ms. Billings, the drama teacher, doesn't seem to be interested in our families. She's too busy with other things. We do a unit on mime, lifting imaginary boxes, being mirrors of one another's actions, playing robots and mannequins and marionettes.

One day she asks me, "Are you taking dance somewhere?"

I shake my head.

"Pity," I hear her say before she moves away to another group. Later, we try some dialogue from plays. She likes the way I speak. One noon hour during Drama Club she has us read parts from a play called *I Remember Mama*, about a new family in America, with a father and a mother and children, three girls and a boy.

"You can read Katrin," she says to me. "Of course she needs to be older in the play, but you sound older, Barbara."

If Livvy and I lived in the *I Remember Mama* world, we would be coming home to a house with supper simmering on the stove, and Mama sitting by the kitchen table, counting out the money Papa has brought home from work in a little envelope, and the people in the family would be joking and teasing one another and thinking about what it would be most important to spend the money on.

Our kitchen is definitely not an *I Remember Mama* kitchen. There is no family chattering. Nothing is simmering on the stove. Through the doorway to the living room comes the sound of the television.

I have told Livvy exactly what she can tell and

what she can't tell when we get home from Cosmo's. "You can tell that you were hit by a bike and a man put some Band-Aids on the places where you got hurt. You can't tell that the man did juggling for us and took us to his place and gave us lemonade. If you do tell, we may not be able to go and see him again. You must promise me Livvy."

Livvy promises.

"Is that you, Barbara?" Daddy calls from the living room.

"Mhmmm."

We're no sooner in the house, of course, when Livvy barrels through into the living room.

"Look, Dad-dee," she dances in, trying to display all of her glow-in-the-dark Band-Aids at once. "I got hit by a bicycle."

Grandma's friend, Mrs. Perth, is over drinking sherry with them and watching a black-and-white movie. Everybody starts clucking and talking at once. "Precious baby. You poor thing. Let's see." They even put the movie on Pause.

"Barbara," Daddy's voice rises above the others. It is his thick afternoon-sherry voice. "Come in here."

I put my survival kit on a kitchen chair.

"What happened to this child? Can't you look after her for a few minutes without her getting run down?"

I start to give the bare facts but no one is very interested. They are fussing over Livvy again.

"I wouldn't let kids of mine out on the streets today." Mrs. Perth puts in her two cents' worth. She looks as old as Grandma Kobleimer and I know her son Myron is older than Daddy. "There's dopers' needles for them to pick up and Lord knows what else. Put up a big fence and keep 'em in the yard."

"Edna, you never said a truer word." Grandma removes the cigarette she's been sucking on. "These streets are getting so it's not safe to set foot out. When Herb and I moved here in '48, kids played all over the place and nobody thought a thing about it. But now, it's a different world..."

"A bicycle accident could happen anywhere," I say. As soon as the words are out I know that I should have kept them to myself and let Grandma go on for half an hour about how great things were in the good old days.

"Barbara, my dear." Grandma cuts each word

amazingly icy and clear, considering how low the sherry bottle is. "That is really not the point. The point is that you and Olivia should not be out roaming the streets. And," she sucks on her king-size Matinee for a couple of seconds, "it maybe isn't my place to comment, but I don't recall you checking with your daddy about taking Livvy anywhere. Of course, I could be wrong."

"Where the hell were you kids?" Daddy gets half out of his armchair, but he's dizzy and slumps back into it.

"I got a ball." Livvy is still dancing around, waving her Band-Aids. "Bingo is his name-o."

"Barbara." Grandma's voice is getting louder. "I believe your father asked you a question."

"We were just at the park."

"Them parks ain't fit for human habitation." Mrs. Perth slurps her sherry, and the creases of flesh in her old neck wobble. "I wouldn't let kids of mine in them for a minute 'less an adult was there in a supervision capacity."

"Did I say you could go to the park?" Daddy screams. "When are you going to learn some responsibility?"

"Kids." Mrs. Perth shakes her head.

"It was just to the park," I say. "We always go to the park."

"Are you sassing your father, missy?" Grandma Kobleimer is struggling to get up with her walker.

"I'm not sassing..."

"See, Bingo's got stars on him, and Cosmo..."

I look daggers at Livvy.

"Oh, oh." Livvy suddenly stops her dancing around. "I gotta go bathroom," she says in her baby voice.

"You mean you already went." Daddy is screaming everything now. "The two of you are going to put me back into the hospital."

"Your poor father." Grandma Kobleimer has raised herself up and her hands are clasped on the walker like the talons of some big bird. "He is this close." She releases the walker with one hand to show a teeny space between her thumb and index finger. "This close to a nervous break-down."

For once it is almost a relief that Livvy has had one of her accidents. "Better go to the bath-room, Livvy."

"Don't think this is finished, missy." Grandma moves her walker along a well-worn route to the bathroom. "I need some time in there first," she says.

"It's okay. I'll take her downstairs. I'll soak the clothes and then give her a bath."

"But my Band-Aids will come off." Livvy starts crying.

"We'll just run a small tub." I tell Livvy to stop her sobbing as I get her out of her clothes. Along with the clothes in the survival bag, there's enough now to do a wash, I think. "You can keep your Band-Aids from getting wet. Then, when you're ready for bed, we can turn out the light and see them glow in the dark."

By the time I have her back upstairs for her bath, Daddy and Grandma and Mrs. Perth are sitting in the silver glow of the black-and-white movie in a kind of trance.

I check the fridge. There is half a loaf of bread and a package of baloney.

"Baloney sandwiches?" I holler.

No one answers except Livvy. "I want mustard and pickles on mine."

"There are no pickles."

"Pooh."

I poke my head into the living room. On the TV, an actress in a Cleopatra headdress is lounging on her barge as it drifts down the Nile. "Baloney sandwiches for everyone?"

"Oh, wouldn't that be lovely." Mrs. Perth flashes her false teeth.

"Mm. Fine," Daddy sighs. "It's too warm to cook anyway."

"You know, they used to say we could have been sisters," Grandma sighs. "Claudette Colbert and me."

In the kitchen, Livvy slathers mustard on half the slices, and we cut the sandwiches into triangles. "Like the pyramids of Egypt," I tell her. "It'll go with their Cleopatra movie."

Livvy and I take our sandwiches out onto the porch to eat. When we're finished, we play catch for awhile in the backyard.

We try to juggle Bingo and a couple of old tennis balls we found. But Livvy is starting to yawn. "Come on, pumpkin," I say. "If you go to bed right away, I'll read to you."

"Can I have a snack?"

"Snack first, and then right to bed."

"I'm having a snack," she announces to the video zombies when we're back inside.

"There's a bag of chips on the cupboard," Daddy says.

"I wish we had lemonade." Livvy is sitting up on the kitchen counter, going into little contortions as she tries to see if all of her Band-Aids are still in place.

Livvy has two beds in her room, bunkbeds side by side. She goes to bed in whichever one is the driest and least smelly. We turn off the lights and pull the blinds down. Her Band-Aids glow faintly, and I hear her sigh with satisfaction. She has a little lamp with dinosaurs grazing around the shade. Mama brought it home one day on her way back from the doctor's. "This was in the window in a Goodwill store," she said. "Can you believe it? All these wonderful dinosaurs?"

When I switch on the light and the dinosaurs glow, I can hear her voice reading me a bedtime story. Livvy was too small to listen. As she slept, she made little baby breathing sounds while Mama read. "You read to her," Mama would say, "when you're older. You're such a good reader."

Tonight Livvy is asleep before I can finish the next chapter of *Charlotte's Web*.

When I go down to take my bath, Cleopatra has finished, and regular TV is chattering away on low volume. Mrs. Perth has fallen asleep and is snoring softly. Daddy has reached his crying stage, his cheeks shiny with tears. Grandma sits with her eyes open, but they don't seem to focus anymore. She sits motionless, most of her cigarette turned to ash, about to fall onto the rug. I hold an ashtray under it and give it a little tap. I hear her voice, no longer loud and demanding.

"Mildred," she says. "Mildred, you should be in bed." Mildred is her daughter who died thirty years ago.

"Your grandma is living in the years gone by," Daddy sniffles. "It's amazing I'm not in the mental hospital with your mama gone, and Grandma slipping away into senile dementia, and Olivia having such problems. Lesser people..." the words lap fuzzily against one another, "lesser people would have just given up. Not many men do what I do. Barbara, honey..."

"Yes, Daddy."

"See if there's another Branvin in the cupboard. I just don't feel like I can get up." I have estimated that Daddy has added ten pounds to his weight with each year since Mama died. He was a big man then, and now he must be close to three hundred pounds.

"Daddy," I say, my voice pleading.

"Well, don't get it then," he snaps. "Lord

knows I don't ask much of you but when I do it's 'Oooh, Dad-dee, don't touch a drink...'" His voice is getting higher and louder. "The pain is more than I can bear, but does anyone care? Oh, yes, it's a different story when the checks come in and Miss Barbara wants a new coat and shoes..." He is yelling at the top of his voice now, stirring Mrs. Perth, pulling Grandma up to the surface of some dream-lake she's swimming in.

I go to the cupboard and bring out the last bottle of sherry and bang it onto the coffee table.

"Well, theeank yeeou," Daddy says, "for the great big favor. Remind me to light a candle for you the next time I'm in church." He winks at Mrs. Perth. "You want a little snort, Edna, before you head for home? That's if Miss Barbara S. Kobleimer has no violent objections."

"I'm going to have a bath," I say, closing the bathroom door on the end of my sentence.

When I sink into the water, I am surprised to find that I have begun to cry. I am suddenly tired beyond belief. I just want to close my eyes and float. If I close my eyes, maybe I can make myself believe I am in the water at Alberta Beach and Mama is saying, "Don't go out too deep, honey. Don't go out beyond your death—" I

51

used to think she said "death" when, of course, she said "depth." When she died, I asked someone, "Did Mama go out beyond her death?" But they didn't understand and said, "No, your sweet mama had a bad cancer running all around inside her. She's out of pain now."

CHAPTER FIVE

Ms. Billings, our drama teacher, also has to teach health. She fills up her health classes with videos on maturation, drug and alcohol abuse. When she runs out of videos, she brings in guest speakers. A nurse from the medical center. A social worker from the school board office. The police.

"Make it a rule not to trust anyone," the police tell us. "You'd be surprised at the smooth talk people might try on you. And it's best not to be by yourself." But does Livvy really count as a second person? It's true she can yell louder than any other kid in our neighborhood. I heard them once at the playground having a screaming competition. No contest.

Plus Cosmo has given us his phone number and told us to tell Daddy and Grandma where we are. He doesn't know that we've told Daddy we're just going to the playground for awhile.

I've explained it all to Livvy, about not saying where we're really going. Actually I think she's not too sure what we are doing. She keeps talk-ing about a curly slide.

"Do you think Bingo will go down the curly slide faster than me?"

"Livvy," I remind her, "we're not going to the park."

"Oh, pooh."

"We're going to Cosmo's. I thought you wanted to go to Cosmo's."

"Will he make lemonade for us?"

"I don't know. But don't ask. It's not polite."

"I can if I want to."

"Don't be a brat."

She sticks her tongue out at me. I knock Bingo out of her hand into some bushes, regret-ting it as soon as I hear her yelling some of the bad words she's heard at the playground and see her down on her knees crawling around a hedge where litter has gathered in a little driftpile. "Don't pick up things from the gutters and the alleys," the nurse from the medical center had warned us. "Sometimes there's used needles..."

"I'll get it," I shout at Livvy.

"No," she yells at me. "Don't touch Bingo. I got him. I don't want you to touch him."

When we get to the landing at the top of

Cosmo's stairs, I let Livvy knock on the door, but no one answers. We lean over the balustrade and look down at the half-crumpled umbrella over the patio table. Red and pink dahlias stare up at us from the garden along the side fence. I can see Livvy is thinking about dropping Bingo over the railing.

"Don't," I say.

"I wasn't going to."

"Were, too."

Livvy retreats into a wicker chair by Cosmo's door. "Can we go to the park?" she grumbles.

Beside the wicker chair there is a funny twisted plant that looks like a little pine tree growing out of a shiny black pot. Bamboo wind-chimes clatter from the eaves.

"Here comes Cosmo now." I see him half-jogging along the sidewalk. The rainbow colors seem to have rearranged themselves. He is wearing a green baseball cap, a sea-blue sweatshirt, pants the color of the marigolds lining the walk below us, and the green sneakers he wore yesterday.

He looks up and sees us. "Hi, guys," he hollers. "Sorry I'm late. Forgot I wouldn't be able to take Mehitabel."

"Cosmo!" Livvy calls down to him. "Catch!" She throws Bingo down. He drops the gym bag he's been carrying and races out of his way to catch the ball. Triumphantly, he waves it in the air. Livvy gives me a smug look.

"So, what are the Kobleimer sisters up to today?" Cosmo asks us when he reaches the landing. "Playing in traffic?"

"No, silly," Livvy laughs. "You want to come to the park with us, Cosmo?"

"Hey, great idea! But let's have a snack first. I'm famished."

"Yay!" Livvy shouts. "Lemonade!"

"If Miss de Havilland would like lemonade, lemonade it shall be." Cosmo reaches behind Livvy's ear and pulls out a house key.

"Hey! How'd you do that?"

"Magic," Cosmo says, giving the door a little kick where it sticks at the bottom. "Welcome to the Emerald City," he says.

The Wizard of Oz is one of the movies Daddy got on an introductory offer to a video club three years ago before he got cut off for not paying for the movies he kept ordering. We've probably watched it a hundred times. We know the Emerald City backwards and forwards.

Cosmo's kitchen looks like it has been stolen from Oz. The walls are a deep green and the windows are covered with green bamboo blinds that are halfway rolled up. The cupboards are still another shade of green, and the wall with a door leading into a living room is covered with pictures of green objects, all overlapping one another. It's a photomontage. We made them in Mrs. Taylor's grade seven art class except this one covers the whole wall.

There is a little wooden table, also green, and two chairs that are the color of the inside part of a watermelon. Cosmo Farber moves around his kitchen with easy, graceful moves, like a dancer. He slides into the living room and puts on some music. It sounds like a piano making raindrops. Then he's back in the kitchen, digging in his fridge. It's a normal white fridge but it has two greenish fish—they must be magnets—swimming across the door.

"So, Miss Olivia de Havilland Kobleimer," he says, "how are those scrapes and bruises mending? You seem to have lost some of your Band-Aids."

"They came off when I was having a bath."

"She was pretty stiff yesterday, but today she's

been skipping all over the place."

"I hope you told your dad how sorry I was." He is cutting a lemon and a lime into slices.

Livvy is squirming on her watermelon chair. I know that if we don't move fast, she'll have an accident. "Can we use your bathroom?"

He nods and points to a door down the hall. We are only a little bit late. I put Livvy's soiled clothes into a plastic bag from the survival bag and help her into the change of clothes I've brought along. She wants to touch all of the things in the bathroom. There's a basket of sponges of different sizes. Not little square ones made out of plastic, but ones that look like they may actually have lived somewhere. There's soap shaped like seashells, some glass prisms hanging in the bathroom window.

"Come on, Livvy," I say. "We can't stay in here forever."

"Aah, metamorphosis," Cosmo says as we return to the kitchen.

I know he means Livvy's change from her Batman top and yellow shorts to her Jurassic Park top and pink shorts.

There are tall drinks for us on the table with ice and slices of lemon and lime and some little sandwiches on see-through plates sitting on placemats that look like big slices of watermelon.

"Mmmm, yummy," Livvy says in her baby-talk voice.

Cosmo dances over to the fridge and brings out three glasses of lemon-colored ice cream. The glasses look like they should be for champagne or some fancy drink, and when he puts them on the table, I see that it's not really ice cream in them.

"Sherbet," Cosmo says, reading my mind again. "The good news," he says, "is you can have seconds. The bad news is the office was all out of brochures for the clown workshop. They're supposed to get some printed in the next couple of days. I think it'll still give you time to get an application in."

At the park, Cosmo and I play ball with Livvy for a few minutes before she decides she needs to test Bingo out on the curly slide. Cosmo and I slip into swing seats, side by side, just barely moving.

"You spend a lot of time looking after Livvy." He says it more as a statement than a question.

"Daddy and Grandma aren't very well."

"So you're chief cook and bottle-washer."

"Daddy used to do more and, when he was working, Mrs. Van Vurstenfeldt used to come in and help. But then we couldn't pay her anymore, and Livvy was getting older, so she could do more things for herself."

"And what happens when you refuse to chief cook or bottle-wash? Or do you ever?"

"Cosmo, look at me!" Livvy shouts from the roof of the little lookout tower by the slide.

"Keep an eye out for pirates," he calls back.

"I just do it," I say. "One time when Mrs. Van Vurstenfeldt first left us, I got mad and went on strike. I hate washing Livvy's clothes. They're always just…yucky. I left them and they rotted and we had to throw most of them out, and then Livvy hardly had anything to wear for awhile. Daddy got really mad…"

I can tell that Cosmo would like to ask some more questions, but I begin pumping my legs to make the swing go higher. There's no easy way to stop a swing once it's in motion, and I close my eyes, letting the sweep up wipe out the image of Livvy's clothes submerged in smelly water in the soaking sink, the plunge down erase the pot of Kraft dinner getting gluey on the stove. I pump away the sound of Daddy being sick when he's drunk too much, and Grandma's rambling conversations with the ghosts of her past. Higher into the sun, the air fresh against my face, and then I let the swing slow down, the arcs getting smaller.

"I want to swing, too." Livvy has wandered over from the curly slide and the monkey bars.

The three of us swing back and forth, and Livvy begins singing her Bingo song. Soon we are all singing it, singing and laughing and pumping our legs, except Cosmo's are too long and he has to just get going and then hold his legs out straight, his green shoes making a path through the air.

"Check it out with your dad," Cosmo says when we reach the gate on the way home. "Day after tomorrow they should have some more brochures. I have a late afternoon meeting, so maybe you can come over just after supper for a little while. Say seven o'clock."

CHAPTER SIX

"**W**here are you off to?" Daddy wanders into the kitchen just as we are about to leave for Cosmo's. He rubs the sleep out of his eyes. He has been sleeping since the middle of the afternoon.

My voice tries to make a sound but nothing comes out. I can't believe I didn't leave five minutes earlier, just after I'd looked in on him and Grandma. But that would have made us a bit early at Cosmo's and I don't want to look over-anxious.

Livvy starts to open her mouth.

"Friends." I find my voice. "Just for a little while."

Daddy holds his head as he gets down to look in the bottom cupboard where he and Grandma keep their sherry. "Don't be late," he mumbles.

I give Livvy a little push.

"Hey, quit it, dodohead."

"Shh." I hurry ahead of her out of the yard.

"What friends?" Livvy asks.

Good question, I think.

At the start of grade six, when Mr. Graydon came to our school, he matched everyone up with a buddy. Buddies kept track of assignments when you were home sick, gave you a birthday card on your birthday, spent time with you on the playground. If parents agreed, buddies visited each other's houses.

I had three buddies in grade six. Tatiana, my first buddy, was at school for only three weeks and then her family moved to Fort MacMurray. Jaycee was my buddy for about six months but she missed more days than she came to school. Mrs. Femeruk told Mr. Graydon it wasn't fair for me to be spending so much time keeping track of Jaycee's homework. Then Jaycee got placed in a foster home and started going to a different school.

Mabel Wong was my last buddy, but we didn't spend much time together. Her grandmother walked her to and from school and showed up at the playground at recess time with little snacks for Mabel. When Mabel tried to share her snacks, her grandmother talked really loud in Chinese and kept waving her hands at me.

By the next fall, when I started grade seven,

we didn't hear anything more about the buddy system. I guess it didn't work that well for most people. I felt kind of sorry for Mr. Graydon.

"Do you spend much time with your friends?" he asked me one time when he got tired of asking me about Daddy and Grandma and Livvy. "You have friends, don't you?"

"Yeah, sure." I could see he was waiting for me to name names. "Tatiana. Jaycee. Mabel." Mr. Graydon gave me a funny look.

Livvy jumps like a rabbit along the sidewalk. "Goodee. Friends," she chants.

"Oh, for heaven's sake, be quiet. We're not going to see friends. We're going to Cosmo's house."

"Cosmo's my friend."

"Okay. But just be quiet."

"You be quiet."

"Grow up." I can see the time on the funeral home clock a block away. It's nearly ten after seven.

"I want lemonade," Livvy sings. "I want green sherbet."

"Don't you say a word about anything to eat or drink, or…" I struggle to think of a good threat. "Or I won't ever bring you with me again."

"Have to."

"Have to what?"

"Have to bring me with you. Daddy says."

She's probably right but I can't let her believe that. "We'll see," I say as mysteriously as possible. "But don't say anything about eating or drinking. Promise."

"But I'm tired of macaroni." It's true. We've been living on macaroni for days. The last of the check money went for a cab to the liquor store. A case of sherry and six previously viewed videos that were on sale for $9.99 each at the video shop.

"Pasta," Daddy says as I cook up pots of macaroni, "is the staff of life in many parts of the world. I could eat it three times a day." At first there was cheese spread to mix into it and, later, a can of tomato soup, but at lunch today it was macaroni and margarine. When Livvy complained, Daddy mixed some ketchup into hers. "There," he said. "Pasta with tomato sauce." Livvy made horrible faces and said "yuckee" a lot, but eventually she ate it.

"Daddy's and Grandma's checks will be in soon, and then we can get some groceries," I tell her. We are in front of Cosmo's house, looking up at the stairs leading to his doorway far above us. "Come on, Livvy," I whisper. "Beat you to the top." She squeals and we clatter up the steps. We are breathless when we get there, and I let Livvy tap on the door.

When Cosmo opens it, I see he is wearing some kind of robe, like a priest might wear in some religion far away. It seems to be made of the colors of sunlight and sand, and it's filled with designs that are a maze, patterns interlocking with other patterns.

"You're wearing a dress!" Livvy exclaims.

"Well, sort of," Cosmo laughs. "It's called a kaftan."

Kaftan. I love the sound of the word. I say it softly to myself.

"It's pretty," says Livvy.

Cosmo has ushered us into his green kitchen and gestures to the watermelon chairs. "I'm just finishing up the dishes. It'll only take a couple of minutes and you can keep me company while I do them." He pulls dishes out of his sink and puts them into a draining rack. The dishes are mostly see-through, and those that aren't are brightly colored yellows, greens, and blues—the colors of the balls he uses for juggling.

Cosmo has opened his refrigerator door. Livvy is hopping from foot to foot and she has grabbed hold of Cosmo's kaftan.

"You two just had supper? Or could you eat some gingerbread and whipped cream?"

"I could," says Livvy before I can stop her.

"How about you, Barbara Stanwyck?"

I feel a flush coming to my face, but I nod. On top of the squares of nut-brown cake, Cosmo spoons a swirl of whipped cream and adds a maraschino cherry to the top of each. Livvy cannot contain herself. She is off her chair, hopping from foot to foot.

"Livvy, do you need to go to the bathroom?" I ask suspiciously.

"No, no, no," she sings. "I love, love, love cherries!"

"Then you shall have two," says Cosmo, adding another to each dish.

"Come into my parlor," he chuckles, a dish balanced in each hand.

We trail through the photomontage arch into his living room. The living room is as white as the kitchen is green. There is no furniture except for large cushions lapping the edge of a rug, and a sound system that covers most of one wall.

There is a window seat built into a small bay, and I sit there, tucking the folds of Mama's crinkled cotton skirt around my legs. The skirt is all shades of pink and red, and I feel that it is one Cosmo will like.

Livvy makes herself a little floor chair by propping one cushion against another.

"Don't you spill anything on those cushions," I tell her while Cosmo ducks back into the kitchen. He comes back with three glasses on a little tray.

"Lemonade," Livvy shrieks.

"You got it."

The gingerbread is soft and moist, and each forkful sends up a flight of spicy smells to my nose. Never in my life have I tasted anything so good. Not even the Oreo cookie blizzards Daddy treated us to on the last day of school when Livvy and I brought home our report cards.

Livvy is making small, contented sounds like a puppy. While we are finishing our plates, Cosmo puts on a CD and presses a couple of buttons on his sound system. The room is filled with soft guitar music. He sits on the floor, cross-legged, his kaftan enveloping his feet.

"So, what have the Kobleimer girls been up to?"

"Not much," I say. "Daddy and Grandma haven't been feeling very well, so I've just..." I search for words, "been kind of looking after things."

"Are they really sick?" Cosmo asks.

"Daddy's having a nervous breakdown," Livvy says.

"Livvy, don't talk about things you don't know anything about," I scold her.

"He is, too. He's this far way," she retorts, holding her fingers the way Grandma does.

"Sorry to hear it," Cosmo says, and there is a little twinkle in his eye.

I don't want to talk about Daddy and Grandma anymore. "We've been reading a lot," I say. "I finished all the books we have from the library. I'll get some new ones tomorrow."

"I want *Charlotte's Web*," says Livvy.

"No, not again," I moan. "Charlotte's died three times already since school let out."

"I love *Charlotte's Web*."

"Well, there are a few thousand other books there as well. We could maybe just see what's in some of them."

Cosmo leaps up suddenly. "I've got it," he says, kind of like Professor Higgins in the *My Fair Lady* movie Grandma and Daddy watch about once a week. "I've been trying to think how I could make amends in some way for running over you, Livvy."

"What! What!" Livvy is clapping her hands.

"I just happen to have a whole boxful of books that my mother sent me when she was cleaning house the other day. All the books I had when I was a kid. You and Barbara shall have them."

"All of them?" Livvy's voice is struck with awe.

"All of them. I'll get them for you before you go and you can take as many as you can carry. And somewhere..." Cosmo is searching here and there, the ledge on top of the fireplace, nooks and crannies of shelves alongside his sound system, the kitchen cupboard counter. "Somewhere I have all the information and the forms for the clown workshop."

"I'll probably have to keep an eye on Livvy," I sigh, pleating Mama's skirt with my fingers. I'm wearing her pink beads as well. They wink at me in the oval mirror on the wall opposite.

"There's a bunch of little bunnies her age doing things at the art gallery. Maybe she could get into a program there while you're in the workshop. I could talk to my friend Bella, or maybe I could convince our director to let her tag along and do some things with us."

"Yes, I want to," Livvy whines.

"I don't know," I say. "Daddy doesn't like us to go very far from home. Livvy's problem, you know…" My voice trails away.

"Problem?" Cosmo asks.

"I want to be a clown," Livvy continues whining.

"It's kind of a bathroom problem."

"They do have bathrooms at the theater and the art gallery," Cosmo says. "Just bring along some extra clothes. And here we are." He finds the papers he's been looking for on a telephone table in the hallway between the living room and his bedroom. "If your daddy can't afford it, there's special funding we can ask for. He'll just need to fill out this part of the form."

"Can I go, Barbara? I want to." Livvy has turned this into a chant.

"I don't know, Livvy. Be quiet."

Cosmo perches some glasses on his nose and

sinks back onto his cushion as he reads the form over. The room has darkened a bit and a floor lamp with a shade pleated like a fan casts a soft light on Cosmo's head. It makes his hair look like spun gold and turns the kaftan an even deeper sun-drenched color. The many shades of gold move as he shifts his position, takes the glasses off, rubs his eyes. For an instant he holds the glasses up against the light, and the long kaftan sleeves fall back, revealing his bandage and the dark bruises on both arms.

"Are those bruises sore?" I ask.

"What, these?" He looks at his arms. "Oh, they're not from the bike accident. It's a kind of skin cancer I have."

Cancer. I can't believe I've made him think about something so awful. I think of the lady at Mama's funeral saying there was cancer running all through her. Sometimes, I guess, it runs along the outside. Is it going to kill you, I want to ask Cosmo, but I can't make my voice say anything.

"I've had it for quite awhile," he says. "It's uncomfortable and sometimes painful, but you get used to it."

I don't know what to say. Livvy has found some little mechanical toys on a shelf and is winding up a pink plastic pig that does a little jig when you set it down.

She squeals with delight.

"Wilbur! Wilbur's dancing!"

"I'm glad you're giving him some exercise," Cosmo laughs. "He likes to dance and he doesn't do it nearly enough."

"Can I have him?" Livvy asks suddenly.

"Livvy!" I scream at her. "That's rude!"

Cosmo puts his index finger across his lips and smiles at me. "You could, Miss Olivia," he says, "if it hadn't been given to me by someone very special. But, tell you what. Whenever you come to visit, you must remember to set him out for a bit of a jig."

"All right," Livvy chuckles.

I want to ask him who gave him the pig, but it's safer to say nothing.

I just listen to Livvy's happy squeals as she sets the pig dancing again, and the CDs of guitar music, and now a lady singing sad songs in a soft, scrapy voice. *God bless the child...* I look more closely at Cosmo's living room. Against the white walls there are shelves with books and knickknacks. Not the china birds and bouquets of flowers and old-fashioned plaster ladies that

Grandma has all over our house, but African animals carved out of wood, oiled and polished, and little boxes of all shapes, some carved, some inlaid with metal and something shiny and white.

One wall is covered with photographs that have frames decorated with patterns of triangles and circles, leaves and flowers. There's a photograph of a clown—it must be Cosmo but I can't be sure—and one of a man with black, curly hair, dressed like someone out of *Romeo and Juliet*. As I look from picture to picture, I realize that the man with the black hair is in most of them.

The pig has wound down and nuzzles its snout into one of the geometric diamonds on Cosmo's rug. Livvy yawns and pats her tummy contentedly.

"I'd better take her home," I say.

"No, me wanna stay," Livvy sighs.

"Books!" Cosmo claps his hands together. "The Kobleimer girls shall not leave, except laden with literature." He disappears and returns dragging a large cardboard box. "I know the perfect one for you, Livvy," he says. "Wilbur is not the only pig to be discovered between the covers of a book. You need to meet Piglet." He rummages and brings out a copy of *Winnie-the-Pooh*. Livvy loves the name. "Pooh, Pooh, Pooh." She dances around, giggling.

"One would think," Cosmo winks at me, "that Miss Livvy has particular associations with that word." He has opened another book. "Oh, hey, you'll like this one, Barbara. *Jane Eyre*. My aunt gave me this, part of a set of classics. I wonder what happened to *David Copperfield*?"

Jane Eyre. I like the sound of it, and I think how wonderful it would be to have a last name like air or westwind or fire, rather than Kobleimer.

"I must warn you that parts of it are sad, and parts of it will make you angry. Do you like *The Secret Garden*?"

"I love it."

"Then you'll like this one, too."

We leave with a bagful of books.

"You can't tell Daddy we have these," I tell Livvy as we walk home, night beginning to soften things in the distance. It is good to be careful of the places where shadows are beginning to pool.

"I want to," Livvy pouts. She is doing a little

dance, and I wonder if she'll get home in time, or if we should have used Cosmo's bathroom before we left.

"If you do, I won't read you any of *Winnie-the-Pooh*."

She considers this threat solemnly. "Okay," she says, "but hurry, I gotta…"

"I know," I say. "We're almost there."

CHAPTER SEVEN

he brochure on the clown workshop
marks the place where I left off reading
Jane Eyre.

Harlequin. Cosmo has told me the name of
the clown in the picture on the cover of the
brochure, an old picture of a figure in diamond
patchwork clothes and a mask. *Find the inner
clown, touch base with the vital force of creativity,
discover the basis for building future experiences in
theater and dance* it says beneath the picture. The
cost is $125. There is a boxed-in square that says
"Funding Subsidy Request." *It is the aim of the
Clown Council that its workshops be available to
all interested candidates...* It goes on for several
lines of small print, followed by a place for a
guardian or parent to sign.

Would Daddy ever sign it?

I read a bit in *Jane Eyre*, but my mind stays on
the workshop. I want to go so badly I feel a kind
of pain across my chest, making it hard to
breathe. With the house quiet, it would be nice

77

to laze in bed, but the tightness makes me restless.

I get up, stopping at Livvy's room. She has had accidents in both of her beds and lies curled up on some pillows on the floor, a blanket half over her. Window squares of light fall on the opened, face-down copy of *Winnie-the-Pooh*, which I read aloud to her until she fell asleep.

I strip the beds and let her sleep. Then I take the bedding and her discarded pajamas down into the basement to the soaking sink. Back up in the kitchen, the morning light shows how dirty the room is. We are out of dish detergent, but I get some laundry soap and tackle the dishes that have piled up over the last couple of days, wiping down the cupboard counter, scraping crumbs out of the cracks, washing the cupboard doors, finally sweeping the linoleum and using what's left of the dish water to give it a wash.

I imagine that I am Cosmo and wonder what he would do at this point.

Flowers.

There's not much in the back yard, but there are patches of daisies along the fence, a bit beaten down from midnight thunderstorms and dust from the alley. But I cut a bunch, wash them in the sink, and find one of Grandma's vases to put them in.

When I check, the coffee canister is empty, but I put the kettle on. Tea will have to do, and Grandma actually prefers it. There is enough of a loaf of bread left to make some toast. I open the tray at the bottom of the toaster, freeing a small mountain of crumbs, add this to the bags of garbage under the sink and then tie these and take them out to the alley.

There are no sounds yet from either Daddy's or Grandma's bedrooms. I make some tea for myself. I let it cool beneath the daisies on the kitchen table, tuck the clown workshop application into the back of *Jane Eyre* and ease into chapter two.

I was a trifle beside myself; or rather out of myself, as the French would say. I was conscious that a moment's mutiny had already rendered me liable to strange penalties, and, like any other rebel slave, I resolved, in my desperation, to go to all lengths.

Jane's words seem stiff and heavy, like carved furniture in a museum, but they are powerful and strong, too. I read the lines over again and sink further into the chapter.

I don't even notice Daddy until he's at the kitchen doorway.

"Pull that shade, Barbara, will you?" He squints against the sunlight. "My eyes have always been too sensitive."

"Morning, Daddy," I say. "Is that why you used to work in theaters?"

"You got it."

I scramble up, pull the blind down, add some hot water to the teapot.

"Angel," he says, settling himself into the other kitchen chair. I put a mug of tea in front of him. He takes it with shaking hands. "Your mother could tolerate the harsh light of day. I never could."

"She liked the sun." I busy myself with the toast.

"I think we'll just turn this into a bit of Long Island Tea." Daddy heaves himself out of the chair and checks the bottom cupboard where he and Grandma keep their bottles of sherry. There is only one left and it is mostly gone. "Oh, well," he sighs. "Maybe Short Island Tea." He pours the last of the bottle into his teacup.

I put the toast in front of him.

"My goodness, such service. And flowers. To

what do we owe all this?"

"Nothing."

But he looks at me sideways.

Livvy, by this time, has wandered downstairs. Like Daddy, she is not a morning person. She stares distrustfully at the bouquet of flowers.

"How's my sweet sugar?" says Daddy.

"I'm tired," says Livvy.

"Maybe we should take her to the doctor again," I say.

"Doctors," Daddy snorts into his tea. "When have they ever been able to help her? Give her a million tests. Give her medicine that won't work. Write down fancy names."

I hear the toilet flushing. Grandma is up. I put more toast in the toaster. "You want some toast, Livvy?"

"I want Froot Loops."

"We're out," I say. "And we're out of milk."

Livvy begins to sob quietly. "I want Froot Loops."

"Well, I want a million dollars." Daddy slams his mug down. "But that doesn't mean I'm going to get it." Livvy puts her head down on the table and cries.

"It's good toast," I say. "And there's some marmalade."

Daddy is eyeing my book. "*Jane Eyre*. Now that was a wonderful movie. Your mother and I saw that when we both worked at the Varsity and they did a series of Orson Welles pictures. Joan Fontaine played Jane Eyre. If we'd had a third daughter, I think we would have called her Joan Fontaine. You know something, pumpkin?" He pats Livvy's snarled hair.

"What?" Livvy inhales between sobs.

"It would have been like real life because Olivia de Havilland and Joan Fontaine were real sisters."

"I want a sister called Pocahontas." Livvy is determined to continue her crying.

I can hear the squeaking of the wheels of Grandma's walker as she makes her way from the bathroom, across the living room to the kitchen.

"Why is that child weeping?" Her voice is full of cracks. "You'd think when I have a migraine…"

"We're out of Froot Loops," I say.

"Don't you cry, Olivia." Grandma fishes her cigarettes out of her bathrobe pocket. Her hands are shaking. She has trouble lighting it, but finally gets the cigarette going, sucks in the smoke. "My check should be in today. The first thing we'll get is Froot Loops."

"Can I have the prize?" Livvy's voice quavers. She knows how to play a scene. It's been years since we quarreled over who got the prize in a package of cereal. I'm surprised she even remembers.

"Of course you can, honey." Grandma darts a look my way. I shrug.

"You want your tea in the living room, Grandma?" If there's one thing Grandma likes, it's to be waited on. She maneuvers her walker around and heads for her armchair.

"I want marmalade toast," Livvy decides.

I make toast for the two of them, scraping the marmalade out into equal portions. Grandma even smiles a bit through the cloud of cigarette smoke as I set a little tray on her end-table, with her tea in a bone china cup and the toast cut in triangles.

"This is lovely, Barbara." She says my name with three distinct syllables. It sounds exotic.

"You go to the bathroom," I tell Livvy when she has wolfed down her toast. "And stay there for five minutes. I'll time you."

"I don't have to."

"Then we can have a game of catch."

"You do what your sister says." Daddy drinks the last of his tea, his hands less shaky.

With just the two of us in the kitchen, I slip the application form from the back of *Jane Eyre* and put it in front of Daddy.

"What's this?"

I tell him about the clown workshop but I don't tell him anything about Cosmo.

"Where'd you get this?"

"At the library."

"You know we don't have any extra money. For God's sake, we don't even have cereal and milk for the baby."

"But you don't have to pay if you sign this part."

He looks at the boxed-in paragraph more closely. "Lord," he says. "They want to know everything from your annual income to the color of your socks."

"Please, Daddy."

"We'll see, hon. I'll have a look at it later. Put it on top of the fridge."

"But it has to be in soon. It starts next week."

"Oh, pee-ardon me. You seem to forget that we have a handicapped child to look after. How many hours a day is this workshop?"

"Three."

"That's a long time for Livvy to go untended if Grandma and I are busy, or not well, or something."

"Maybe Livvy could come along."

"You know she can't be far away from home."

"Why—"

"Barbara, I will look at this later. Now put it away. I think Grandma wants some more tea."

Now I am crying, but I face the cupboard and won't let him see me. He wanders into the living room and I hear the television click on.

"What would you like to see, Mom?"

"Oh, you know me," Grandma says. "Anything you like is fine with me. Do we have any Claudette Colbert? People used to say I looked like her." I hear the sound of a cassette being sucked into the VCR and a swell of movie-studio music.

◆

Grandma's check does come in the mail. Which means we will all be heading down to the bank in a taxi and then over to the grocery store and the liquor mart. I help Grandma into her going-out dress. It is a deep rose pink with a pattern of splashy flowers. I hook the buttons along her back. It seems like each time I do it, her back has curved even more into a stoop. Livvy has changed into her party dress even though it needs cleaning. She spilled orange pop on the lace when Grandma's money came in last month.

"Pretty, pretty," Livvy chants, twirling around.

"You got a change of clothes for her, Barbara?" Grandma asks.

Livvy and I squeeze into the back seat of the taxi beside Daddy, who has shaved and patted his cheeks and neck with after-shave. The layered smells of alcohol and perfume fill the car. Grandma sits stiffly in the front seat clutching her shiny black purse.

When we pull up to the bank, Daddy gets out and helps Grandma. It is hard for her to walk without her walker.

"I want to go in, too," Livvy pouts.

"You kids wait in the car and be good," Daddy calls back at us.

"Guess what I've got here." I pat the survival bag. Livvy's attention is easily captured.

"Candy?"

"No. Nothing that will rot your teeth." I

reach in and fish out *Winnie-the-Pooh*.

"Oh, goodee." Livvy claps her hands. She smiles and waves at the reflection of the taxi driver's face in the rear-view mirror. As I continue with the chapter where Piglet meets a Heffalump, she sighs and leans back into the seat, but it is hard to keep her attention with the radio crackling and bursting into messages.

"We got money," she sings when Grandma and Daddy return.

"And we know who wants to spend it," Grandma cackles as she struggles back into the seat. "You can take us to Mama Isabella's," she directs the taxi driver.

"Goodee, goodee, goodee. Pizza! I want pineapple."

"What do you want, Barbara?" Daddy asks.

I want to go to the clown workshop, I think, but I say, "I'll share Livvy's pineapple one. I like pineapple." It will be good to have pizza after all the macaroni we've been eating, but at the same time I'm dreading the hours that stretch ahead.

Mama Isabella's is tucked in between the liquor mart and the Safeway. It is hard to get Daddy and Grandma away from a booth at Mama Isabella's. When we're finished the pizza,

I try playing hangman on the paper placemat with Livvy, choosing a really easy word to spell—DOG—but she decides to take over and draw the man on the gallows. Daddy and Grandma have finished the wine they've had with supper and are on their third Irish Cream when Daddy tells Livvy and me to go to the Safeway and load up the grocery cart.

Livvy has managed to spill tomato sauce all down the front of her dress. "I want to push the cart by myself," she says. She has already banged into a pyramid of canned corn, and the man at the cigarette counter is watching us out of the corner of his eye.

"Okay," I say. "But you have to be really careful, and you have to stay behind me."

"Oh, bah. Baa, baa, baa."

"Livvy."

"It's not any fun."

"Grocery shopping's not supposed to be fun."

"Baa."

"Are you a sheep?"

Livvy giggles.

We go up and down the aisles. Froot Loops. Milk. I have a hard time getting Livvy away from the bakery department. She piles a chocolate cake and strawberry tarts into the cart.

"Grandma will get mad," I tell her.

"Baa," Livvy says. "Can we go home now? Me wanna play with Bingo."

"Just a bit more."

The cart is piled full and we have done two word-search puzzles, waiting on the bench by the door, when Daddy and Grandma finally come. They have been arguing. Daddy's cheeks are wet with tears, and Grandma's mouth is a tight, thin line.

"Daddee." Livvy hangs onto Daddy's trousers. "I need to whisper something to you."

"Did you have an accident?"

"No," Livvy scowls. He bends down, and when she's through whispering, he says, "Ask Grandma. It's her check."

"Can we get a chocolate bar?" Livvy acts suddenly shy and looks as if she is going to burst into tears. "And can I get a Pocahontas coloring book?"

Grandma Kobleimer has eased herself into a chair by the door. "Get whatever you want. My money isn't my own these days."

We stop at the video store and Livvy pulls six movies off the shelves before we notice what she's up to. Daddy has already piled my arms full from the Classics section.

"*Carnosaurs. Interview With a Vampire.* Are you out of your mind, child?" Daddy hollers.

"How come I never get to choose?" Livvy is sobbing now, more from fatigue than anything else.

"*Child's Play 2.* Every one of these needs to be put back."

"The children's section is over by the window," I say. "Maybe you can choose a couple from there."

"I want to go home," Livvy cries. It's too late to get her to a bathroom, I realize. Daddy shoves Livvy's videos onto the nearest shelf.

"Oh, for crying out loud. Couldn't you have waited a few more minutes till we got home."

Daddy's voice is rising all the time. I see people looking at us sideways. Livvy has broken into loud sobs. Daddy pulls some bills out of his pocket and tells me to pay for the videos while he gets Livvy out to the taxi.

"Looks like your dad took out the whole Classics section." A boy with three earrings in one ear and two in his nose punches in the movies. "*Titanic.* Never knew there was an old movie of that."

The taxi driver takes some more of Grandma's money when we get home. His nose is wrinkled up and he mutters, "There better not be any damage to my upholstery," as Livvy climbs out of the back seat.

"You ever heard of a tip?" Daddy asks him, his voice tight.

"Whaddya mean?"

"I mean you aren't going to *see* one. Your precious upholstery is filthy to begin with."

"That upholstery was shampooed…"

I start to lug the groceries out of the trunk.

It is close to an hour later by the time I've helped Livvy get ready for bed. She is so tired she barely touches the piece of chocolate cake she insisted on for a snack, and falls asleep before I can finish a page of *Winnie-the-Pooh*. It's hot in her room, and her curls lie damp against her face. For a time I sit and look at her. There is a faint smell of perfume from the soap she used in her bath and didn't do a very good job of rinsing off. That and the bathroom smell that is always in her mattresses, stronger in the heat. She sighs in her sleep and mumbles something about Bingo. From downstairs I can hear the drone of the television and Daddy's voice above it.

"No man was ever expected to put up with what I have to," he is half-hollering, half-crying.

"Pipe down," Grandma screeches back.

Raindrops on roses and whiskers on kittens, a voice swells from the TV as they both pause for breath.

•

I slip downstairs past the hollering and crying and *The Sound of Music* and get the clown workshop application from the top of the fridge. There are other forms there. Government welfare forms, a couple with Daddy's signature. I take them along with *Jane Eyre* and go back to my room.

This is the smallest room in Grandma's house. Mama used to do sewing in it, her hands guiding pieces of cloth across the work leaf, the chatter of the needle mixing with the sound of a little radio she carried with her from room to room, while I played with a doll or did a word search on the floor.

"This will be a blanket to wrap my baby bunting in," she would sing softly. Livvy was curled up inside her, growing bigger week by week. "And this…" She would pull a piece of cloth out of a big cardboard box filled with odds and ends of material. "This will be a sundress for

—
92

your dolly, to match our own." Mama liked to dress the two of us in matching outfits. Complete strangers would come up to us and say things like, "Aren't the two of you a picture," and Mama would laugh and show all her crooked teeth.

"We are," she'd say. "We are."

The sewing machine has been broken for years, but with its work leaf closed over the top of the cabinet, I can use it as a desk. I work through the form: address, telephone (I put in a dash), annual income (I write "unemployed," and then, with a slash, "welfare"). There is a place for additional comments. I try different ways of saying it on a piece of paper, and then I write: *My current financial circumstances make it impossible for my daughter to get into a program like this, but she has a strong interest, and we have always been a family interested in theater*. Daddy's signature is not easy to copy and I write it about thirty times before signing E. A. Kobleimer on the dotted line. My hand is trembling at this point, but the form is filled in. I fold it and slip it into the back of *Jane Eyre*.

I feel sick to my stomach.

When I crawl into bed and try to read, I can't

concentrate. Lies and forgery. I have told lies and committed forgery. What would Cosmo think?

Or Mama? I try turning off the light and going to sleep but that doesn't work either. I get up and get a glass of water and drink it sitting at the sewing machine in the dark. My window will only push up a little way before it sticks, but it's enough to let in a bit of night breeze. It feels good against my face, and I press the cold glass of water against my cheek.

The outside night is filled with little spots of sound. A baby crying a few houses away, and a cat yowling but far enough away you can barely hear it, a car with its radio on moving slowly along the street. There is enough light from the streetlight for me to see the photographs I have tacked to the wall by the sewing machine: Mama and Daddy's wedding picture, Mama smiling with her big teeth, Daddy with a moustache and his hair dark and shiny; one of Mama holding me as a baby; a family photo of all of us, Livvy a few months old on Mama's lap, already Mama's face looking thin and bones showing that you can't see in the other pictures.

"Oh, Mama," I say, so softly it is just a little whisper in the night air. "I'm sorry."

osmo is heading off on his bicycle when I take the form over after we've eaten breakfast the next morning.

"How's Mehitabel?" Livvy asks, bouncing Bingo on the sidewalk. She's getting so she can catch it on the rebound.

"Mehitabel is as good as…better than new. I treated her to a new coat of paint after I got the wheel fixed."

"Pret-tee," Livvy pats a shiny red piece of the frame and practices ringing the bicycle bell.

"Here's the clown workshop form. Daddy says I can go if I take Livvy along." I can feel my face growing hot with the shame of the lie.

"Hey, great. Wonderful." Cosmo gives me a wide smile and winks at Livvy. "My friend Bella can let her paint for the last part of her workshop, and then she can come at break time and we'll find something for her to do."

"I want to be a clown, too."

"You're already a clown," Cosmo laughs.

"See you guys on Monday."

We watch Cosmo and Mehitabel disappear down the street.

"You'll like painting," I tell Livvy. "Remember the ones you did at school and we had on the fridge?"

For Christmas last year, Livvy's teacher gave all of her students smiling Santa fridge magnets and Livvy began putting up the pictures she'd painted at school.

"My family," she announced, pinning up a picture with four figures, including an almost-round man with a bottle in one hand and a TV remote in the other. It disappeared overnight once Daddy took a close look at it. That left the one with children and elephants playing together on the playground until Livvy decided she needed the fridge magnets to stick to the monkey bars at school.

"Mrs. Foster says I paint elephants really good." Livvy talks nonstop as we walk downtown on Monday. "And I can do alligators better than Josh, most of the time. One time he did one better."

I shift the survival bag to my other hand. It is fifteen blocks, and I switch it every three blocks.

In it there is a change of clothes for Livvy in a plastic grocery bag, some sandwiches, although we ate just before leaving, one of my school scribblers with its used pages torn out, in case we need to take notes, the new word-search book I slipped into the grocery cart at Safeway, *Jane Eyre*, *Winnie-the-Pooh*.

When I take Livvy into the children's workshop in the art gallery across from the theater studio, Cosmo's friend, Bella, gives her a big hug and I know she will be okay. Her attention has already been caught by the gigantic pieces of paper unrolled over the floor. Kids have begun to paint a mural of people parading along on bicycles and skateboards and roller-blades.

"You can work with Walden." Bella gestures to a boy who says, "Hey, can you paint some people running? I want people running in front of these kids walking a dog."

"I want to paint a dog," says Livvy.

"Okay," says Walden. "We need more dogs."

I give Bella the grocery bag with the change of clothes. "She might need these."

"Yes, Cosmo told me. Now don't you worry—and I'll walk her over to the acting studio when we're finished." Bella gives me a little hug, too. She is a hugging sort of person with bright hair and lipstick, and a pile of jewelry. "Have fun."

Fun. My nerves seem to be having a jumping contest in my stomach. "Come in the side door of the theater," Cosmo had instructed me. But I'm not sure if I can walk across the street and open the door and let myself into this whole new world. When I do move, it is like I'm a zombie.

The workshop room is a small amphitheater with kids clustered here and there on the seat steps leading down to the stage. There are three girls in a pool of backpacks, their hair in fluorescent colors: turquoise, purple, red. A tall, gangly boy with no hair at all, his shaved head shining under the lights, is sitting off by himself reading a book. Two other boys lounge against a pillar, their quiet talk broken now and then with hoots of laughter. One has dark, curly hair tied back in a ponytail. The other looks like someone in a Gap clothing ad.

A girl in a black leotard is going through some kind of series of exercises. Maybe she's a ballet dancer. She lies down on one of the terrace levels and slowly raises a leg toward the ceiling.

From across the room, an overweight girl with a lumberjack shirt tied around her waist watches her.

Suddenly I am aware that someone else has come in and is standing beside me. I try not to look at him but he starts talking to me right away.

"Hey, is th...this...th...the clown workshop?" he struggles.

"Yes." My voice comes out as a little croak. "Yes, I think so," I say louder. He is part Native, with dark hair to his shoulders.

"Good." He smiles, flashing his teeth. "I've been all over th...th..." He pauses and takes a breath. "...this building." He is wearing a small gold earring. His skin is a dark tan spotted with pockmarks and pimples. He drops his backpack and stretches his arms. I set the survival bag beside it.

From one of the side entrances, Cosmo comes onstage. He's wearing one of his outfits of many colors along with a red clown nose, and he moves slowly across the stage, lost in his own thoughts. We are all watching him. The overhead lights pick up the spun gold of his hair. Suddenly he stops, as if he has only just become aware of us, smiles and waves us down to the stage. In a couple of minutes he has us all down there, sitting cross-legged in a circle.

Cosmo begins talking, but all I can hear to start with is a kind of buzzing in my ears. It's like all the blood in my body has suddenly made a mad dash for my head. Rush hour in the arteries. I take a deep breath. "That's it," Mama would say when she was teaching me to swim. "Just take a big breath and hold it inside you and you won't drown. You'll be just like an inner tube bouncing around on the water."

When I let my breath out, the buzzing in my ears has settled down into a soft, fuzzy sound.

"There is a clown inside all of us," Cosmo is saying. I feel he has been watching me for the last couple of minutes.

"It is the spirit that we have inside us when we're children. The love of play, the wonder of discovery."

It seems odd to see Cosmo away from his green kitchen, a teacher instead of a lemonade-maker, instead of the person on the swing set singing *Bingo is my ball-o*.

"Part of the purpose of this workshop is to develop ways to keep this childlike sense of joy close by," Cosmo is saying, "as a kind of lifesaver. Picture yourself threshing away with problems and pressures. You have a twenty-page social studies paper to turn in tomorrow and it's already ten o'clock at night. Your boyfriend tells you he needs more freedom and maybe you should quit going steady. Your dad has decided you should work in the hardware store for a year instead of enrolling in fine arts at college. You grab hold of your clown life-preserver and it helps you float through."

He passes around a bag of clown noses for us to put on. We are to introduce ourselves by giving our name and telling about a time when we were younger and everything felt good. The best time in our life.

"Close your eyes," Cosmo says, "and I'll start."

I close my eyes. The plastic nose pinches and makes me want to sneeze. Someone coughs and somebody else giggles. I have an urge to giggle myself, but now it is totally quiet.

"My name is Cosmo the Clown. This is a name I have chosen for myself." Cosmo begins. "My parents hadn't figured out who I really was when I was born so I went through the first part of my life with the name Garson Farber. You can see it really did need to be changed." There is a little sputtering of chuckles around the circle. "The time I am thinking of is when I was about ten years old. I spent a month with my Aunt Charity in an old farmhouse in the Okanagan."

Cosmo's voice is very soft. We have to listen hard to hear everything he is saying.

"It was August and we ran through orchards and gathered apples." He stops and it is as if he somehow has those apples in front of him, in his hands. "Some of them we made into thick, juicy pies, some into apple cider, some into funny old people with wrinkly apple faces."

He laughs softly, holding the sound in the back of his throat. "Apple people. Then we dragged a puppet theater out of the attic and made about twenty puppet characters out of worn-out socks, and made up plays. We dressed ourselves each day out of a costume box and rolled on the floor laughing as we looked at each other in different hats."

The boy with the stutter has moved up close to me. An overhead light catches a shiny part of his earring.

"Each night, Aunt Charity read to me out of

her favorite books, and I would go to sleep in a warm upstairs room that smelled of cedar wood and mothballs, to the sound of my aunt's voice."

Cosmo's own voice has almost faded away into the still air. "Who'd like to go next?"

The earring on the boy has quit winking at me. When I steal a look, I see he has sprawled down, totally, on the floor. And he's looking up at me.

The girl with the lumberjack shirt raises her hand. "My name is Jessica-Marie Daniels and my most perfect time was when I was about eight years old and my dad was still with us." The words come in a rush and Jessica-Marie stops and catches her breath. "He was a little bit crazy but he liked playing with us kids and, for a Christmas holiday, we had a cabin at a ski lodge. It was too cold to ski and we stayed inside by the fire and played a game he invented called Magic Lines where one person would draw a squiggle and the next person had to make the squiggle into part of a picture. I was the best. I could make squiggles into just about anything. And my dad laughed and laughed, and even my mom cracked a smile or two."

I don't want to go last, so after the girl with

the turquoise hair tells about how her best time was riding horseback on a guest ranch near Hinton, I recite my Alberta Beach memory. I can barely hear myself to start with, but my words get stronger and louder as I go on.

The Native boy is next. He stutters when he says his name, Nathan Meredith, but once he is telling us about his best time, the stuttering almost disappears. "I r-remember when my grandpa took me up to his cabin near St. Paul. It's a cabin on a lake and we went fishing every day and made bannock and ate fresh jackfish, and he would tell me stories, you know, about the Indian way, and when he was a young man. He liked to play jokes a lot, and we would split a gut...you know, laughing, and then..." He pauses and a choke comes into his voice. "And th...then, my m...mom figured out where we were and came and got me. But it was good for awhile..." His voice trails off.

"That's great." Cosmo has lifted himself to a half-crouch in front of us. "All of you have pretty good life-preservers. Use them, like I say, when you're feeling blue, or you feel like you're being driven over very slowly by one of those big rollers they use for smoothing pavement."

He flashes a goofy grin. "We're just going to limber up a bit now." He has us become rag dolls and then mannequins. While we're doing that, he drags in a wooden trunk filled with things like scarves and gloves and different kinds of hats. We are to each choose one thing that catches our fancy.

"Look at the color of the item. How does it make you feel? When you put it on, let the color change how you feel. Let the object guide your behavior. I'll begin." Cosmo leaves the trunk open and walks to the edge of the stage. He returns slowly, as if he is incredibly tired, almost tripping over the trunk. He looks at us with an expression of surprise and then it changes into one that is filled with excitement and wonder as he discovers different items: a pink scarf that he lets drift along his face, a beanie that makes him smile stupidly. Finally he settles for a pair of yellow gloves which he puts on slowly, shivering as he smooths the cloth over his fingers. Once they are on, he becomes filled with energy, electric, dancing around, waving his hands like a dancer, then keeping an imaginary ball afloat, then being a traffic policeman.

Cosmo crooks his finger and nods toward the

trunk. The kids all gather around him and everybody seems to make a quick choice. When I stand up, I feel my legs begin to shake.

"Go ahead and jump, sweetie," Mama would holler when she was trying to get me to dive. "You can swim like a fish. Now you just need to learn to dive. You can do it. I'm right here."

I would look down from the diving board to where Mama was below me, her hands reaching up. I wanted to get on my hands and knees and crawl back.

I have the same feeling now. I wish there were some way I could disappear. This is different than grade seven drama. There it was like everyone was in the beginners' class. Here I can see kids who look like they're training for the drama Olympics.

I have a feeling that Nathan Meredith isn't ready to rush up and get something out of Cosmo's trunk, either. We are the last ones. Cosmo spills the remaining props out so we can see them. There is a corsage of white flowers, the kind that college boys give to their prom dates in the movies. There's an old-fashioned handbag all covered with sequins and beads. There's a cowboy hat and a balaclava and a lady's straw sunhat with a green ribbon tie.

"Do any of these make you think of anything?" Cosmo asks.

"Uh—I'll t-take this." Nathan picks up the balaclava. "I l-lost mine after I robbed the S-Seven Eleven last week."

The sunhat makes me think of an old movie called *Gone With the Wind* that Daddy and Grandma watch every couple of months. There's a beautiful girl in the movie and she goes to a barbecue in her hoop skirts and a big sunhat. She flirts with all the young men and makes their girlfriends jealous. Maybe if I take the sunhat I can turn myself into the beautiful lady.

Cosmo smiles at me and nods.

I take the sunhat over behind a pillar where nobody can see me. What do I do with it now? Do I just put it on and become a beautiful belle?

There needs to be something more.

Sometimes, when we had a few minutes left at the end of a drama class, Ms. Billings would pop a tape of Carol Burnett skits into the VCR and we would watch them. What would Carol Burnett do? I think of her cleaning lady act and I decide that's what I'll do, be a cleaning lady who's working in a theater prop room where she finds the hat and then turns into a gorgeous lady. Besides, I've done the cleaning lady twice already in drama skits at school.

When it comes time for people to show what they've come up with, everyone goes before Nathan and me. The girl who looks like she's a ballet dancer does a dance, like a Japanese geisha, with the paper fan she chose from Cosmo's trunk. The boy with the ponytail tucks his hair up under a black beret and pretends he is playing an accordion at a restaurant.

When it's his turn, Nathan puts the balaclava on the lid of the trunk. He moves around the stage, timid, frightened. But when he finds the balaclava and puts it on, he is suddenly powerful, forceful, dodging back and forth like a boxer, doing Ninja kicks.

When he is finished, I grab my imaginary bucket and mop and move like a tired old woman onto the stage.

"Wonderful," Cosmo praises us. He brings out a cooler of juice and a container of cookies. "Time for a bit of a break now," he says.

On cue, Bella arrives with Livvy, who is dragging a large sheet of paper.

"Hey, look, Cosmo," she says. "I did the best

elephant. It was going to be a dog but then I made it into an elephant."

"Wow," says Cosmo. "And you're just in time for cookies and juice."

Some of the other kids are standing around us, and Livvy, never bashful, displays her picture for each of them. For the last half of the workshop, she nibbles cookies on the upper terrace and draws on a piece of manila Bella has left with her—an elephant friend for the one she has painted.

"So, what do you think?" After the workshop, Cosmo walks with us as far as his house, wheeling Mehitabel alongside. "You were good, Miss Barbara Stanwyck. Great with the sunhat."

"It was fun. A little scary, but fun."

"I was great with my elephant," Livvy reminds him. She has the large papers rolled with a rubber band around them.

"You were," Cosmo laughs. "Bella says you're a natural." We are at Cosmo's yard. "See you tomorrow," Cosmo waves at us.

"You can't let Daddy see your pictures," I tell Livvy.

"I want to show him and Grandma."

"It needs to be a surprise for later. If he asks

where we were, you have to say we were at the playground and the library."

"Oh, bah."

"Yes, bah. Promise me, Livvy. It's really important."

She scowls at me.

"Promise. Or I'll never play ball with you again, or read you *Winnie-the-Pooh*."

"Can we play with Bingo when we get home?"

"If you promise."

"I promise," Livvy sighs.

Daddy and Grandma are both asleep when we get back to the house. The end of a videotape runs bright blue on the screen. I make a game of tiptoeing around the house with Livvy, getting her to the bathroom, putting her pictures up in her room, finding Bingo from where she's let him roll under the bed.

We are playing ball in the back yard when Daddy finally appears at the kitchen door. "Barbara," he says, "we have five videos to take back. You and Livvy go for a little walk and tell them we want a two-day extension on the others."

"I'm tired of walking," Livvy says.

"What do you mean?" Daddy has come out

onto the back porch, shielding his eyes against the afternoon sun.

I catch Livvy's eye and shake my finger at her.

"It won't hurt you both to get a little exercise. My, this heat is something. I think we'll just have cold cuts and potato chips for supper."

"And chocolate cake," Livvy sings out.

"Chocolate cake. But do your errand first. There's a dollar for each of you to buy something you want."

"Yippee!" Livvy dances around, clapping her hands.

CHAPTER NINE

The second day of the workshop, Cosmo gathers us in a circle again. One of the girls with day-glo color in her hair—fuchsia, she told us in the washroom—has detached herself from the other two and positioned herself as close to the bald boy—Scott—as it is possible to be without actually touching him. The girl who had bright red hair yesterday is neon green today. Her name is Cloud. "My best time," she told us yesterday, "was when I went to a Smashing Pumpkins concert with my girlfriend and we met these guys, like real cool, who thought we were about three years older than we really were."

The boy with his hair in a ponytail, Roger (but say it Roh-zhay, he announced yesterday), is wearing cut-off jeans and sits cross-legged, his tan legs gleaming in the overhead light.

"Do you think he shaves them?" Jessica-Marie nudges me with her elbow. I wonder if she has somehow read my mind.

"This afternoon," Cosmo says, "I want to spend just a bit of time on the whole business of where clowns come from." He is dressed all in black today, loose-fitting cotton and black slip-on shoes like the Chinese wear. He begins by asking us all where we first saw a clown.

"M-Me," Nathan says, "I got put into a barrel by a clown when I was about three years old. It was at a rodeo and the b-barrel had a really stinky smell and I started howling my head off. My mom socked him, I think. She didn't like for anyone to make me cry unless it was her."

Nathan is beside me, leaning back on his elbows, the rest of his body slung forward. He has a rumpled look, as if he's slept in his clothes.

Most of the kids say the circus or the Exhibition parade. I have never been to either. Some years there were circus tickets given to us at school, but we still had to be taken. At first Daddy was too busy working weekend afternoons and evenings, and then, when he quit work, he never wanted to leave the house unless it was to cash his welfare check, go for pizza or do the shopping. "Watch *The Greatest Show on Earth*," he would say. "It's better than going to the circus and running to the bathroom every ten minutes with little miss you-know-who."

"Jimmy Stewart," I tell the group. "The clown in *The Greatest Show on Earth*. It's an old movie my dad taped off the late show."

"Ah, yes," Cosmo says, bringing out a little wicker suitcase. "The wanted man, the misfit hiding behind a false nose and greasepaint. Probably one of the more interesting aspects of the clown—the painted face, the mask—and one we'll be working with later today." With the cover sprung open, we can see the suitcase is filled with clippings, brochures, magazine photos.

I think of the cardboard box hidden way back under the sewing machine at home. Mama's collection is in it. She has every picture of Jimmy Dean that she could find when she was a teenager. "I would trade Elvis pictures for Jimmy Dean," she'd tell me when we spread the pictures out on the sewing-room floor. "Wasn't he handsome? I had twice as many as Marilyn Marsden." Sometimes I take them out and look at them when Livvy isn't around. She ripped the heads off six Jimmy Deans one time, so I'm careful to keep the box hidden. James Dean is sad, though. Even when he's smiling.

"Pierrot," Cosmo says, holding up a clipping of a figure with a painted white face and a sad expression like James Dean, in clothes something like Cosmo's own, black with white pompom buttons. There are pictures of the other Italian clown figures, Harlequin and his girlfriend Columbine, and her scheming father Pantaloon. There is a scene of the jester and the king from King Lear. "The clown was important in a world where even the rich and the powerful lived close to death, close to the changing tides of fortune," Cosmo says.

There are other pictures. Cosmo shows them to us one by one, as if they were his family album. Nathan, I can see, is watching me again, rather than Cosmo. He has a puzzled look, as if he's trying to figure out what I am thinking. He lounges back in the middle of the sprawl of clippings.

"Maybe the clown is a mirror," Cosmo is saying, but he seems to have lost us. It's as if he is, in fact, looking into a mirror. "A mirror," he says again, "into which we look, not straight on, but kind of out of the corner of our eye."

Cloud, checking the spikes in her hair, gives an audible little sigh and Cosmo shakes himself like someone working his way out of a dream. "But enough reflection," he grins at us. "Clowning is all about movement and action and expression. For the next half hour I want you to work with a partner, just to bounce ideas off one another. Try some little bits of action, mime moves, business that might possibly be built into a clown character."

Partners. As Cosmo goes on with instructions for the exercise, I look around. Nathan wiggles an eyebrow my way, but Jessica-Marie is already tapping me on the shoulder. "You want to work together? I think I'm going to be somebody who's awesomely clumsy. I'm already pretty good at it."

"Sure," I say, giving Nathan an I'm-sorry look.

As it turns out, Nathan and his partner, Cloud, attach themselves to Jessica-Marie and me. Cosmo has said we can go anywhere close by to practice, and the four of us end up in a park across from the theater. Both Cloud and Nathan are smokers, and Jessica-Marie is an out-doors freak, making sure she is upwind from the nicotine addicts.

Nathan decides to be a character who mimics

whatever he sees, flapping his arms like a seagull, bouncing up and down like a puppy. Cloud thinks he's hysterical. The crazier he gets, the more she shrieks with laughter, taking breaks to drag on her cigarette or re-apply her vampire-red lipstick.

Jessica-Marie has decided to add compulsive eating to her clumsy routine, consuming everything in sight: leaves, paper plates, an abandoned running shoe. She is pretty funny, and we're all giggling by the time she has finished plucking bits of velcro from between her teeth.

I pretend I'm afraid of just about everything in the world. When I open a discarded pizza box, it's like the *Nightmare on Elm Street* has been waiting inside. When I see my reflection in a mirror, I nearly faint from the shock. Nathan gives me a high five when I've done a few minutes of this.

Cloud mainly just wants to smoke and watch us. Finally she decides she will be someone who goes around acting like a three-year-old. Nathan lets her hang onto him as if he were her older brother.

It is a warm afternoon and people come and go in the park. A crew is setting up a stage and some tents. One of the workmen applauds as we finish our routines. We all turn and give him the actor's stage bow. Nathan bums a cigarette off Cloud for a quick smoke before we head back. Cloud lights up one as well.

"So, Cloud, you gonna be a clown when you grow up?" Jessica-Marie has flopped down on the grass.

"Fun-nee." Cloud makes a face at her. "I think I'll be kind of a model-actress, you know, some modeling in ads, and maybe act in a series. My mom thinks I should go on the stage." She says the words as if she's bitten into something that tasted bad. "So she has me taking ballet and going to the fine arts high school and everything, but I don't want to go to university and study Shakespeare. Yuck." She says yuck the same way Livvy does. "She's enroled me in every drama workshop that's come along since I was twelve years old."

"F-For the last two years, th-then," Nathan teases.

"Fun-nee. I happen to be seventeen." She blows a little series of smoke rings.

"Wow," says Jessica-Marie, watching the small donuts of smoke drift away and disappear.

"You got hidden talents."

"Of course I could've got out of this work-shop if I'd wanted to. All I'd have had to do was tell my dad the instructor has AIDS and that would've been it. He freaks out when you say AIDS."

I watch Cloud's mouth as it keeps moving, words and smoke drifting out and hovering around us, but my mind has stopped. I close my eyes and see the young man Ms. Billings had in as a guest speaker in our health class. Adam something, looking like one of those prisoners they found in the concentration camps at the end of World War II, like a skeleton, his hair cropped. But he smiled and told us about living with AIDS and what you could do to try not to get it.

Cosmo.

Nathan is tapping me on the arm. "T-Time we got back," he says.

I see the kids leaving the art gallery, and holler across at Livvy.

"Hey, Barbara," she calls back from the corner, "guess what!"

"What?" I say. We all wait for her on the corner.

"You know Walden, the one I was painting with. Well, he said I was stinky so I painted his dog's face blue, and he got mad at me and hit me, and I punched him and I knocked the blue paint over and it got on my shorts. So that's how come I'm wearing my red shorts, but I didn't have an accident."

"What did Bella say?"

"She got mad at both of us. Walden and I both had blue paint on us. She said we looked like the war guys in some place where they paint themselves blue when they go out fighting. Then she started laughing."

Inside the theater, Livvy's story ends abruptly when she sees Cosmo handing out cold drinks along with crackers and cheese.

"Mm," she says, "me hungry." Livvy finishes off the tray of crackers as we begin sharing what we came up with before the break. Then I see her curl up on the seat-steps, using someone's backpack as a pillow.

When we are through sharing, Cosmo has us make a circle again. He is sitting cross-legged along with us. Using his little wicker suitcase as a table, he has opened a makeup box.

"Next week," Cosmo says, "we are going to

begin creating our own individual masks. This week, I want to look at face paint and what can be done with that." His fingers sift through an assortment of bottles and tubes, greasepaint sticks, makeup pencils and brushes, toothpicks, Q-tips and tissues. There is gold and silver in little bottles like druggists use for medicine. Cloud looks more interested than she has all day.

"A clown takes great pride in the way he creates his face with paint," Cosmo says. "Some have actually registered their designs—kind of like a copyright."

He has taken the white grease pencil and begun working it along his forehead just below his hairline. "First I am making my face totally white with a greasepaint stick called Clown White. White, of course, shows up from a distance."

As Cosmo makes his face whiter and whiter, I feel like he is beginning to disappear. I'm glad when he takes a black pencil and draws a line where the clown white meets his unpainted skin, stopping the white from spreading any farther.

"White," Cosmo says, "picks up the light, and it creates something of a blank page on which we can write any expression in the eyebrows, the eyes, the outline of the mouth."

Looking into the mirror on the lid of the makeup case, Cosmo carefully arcs two black lines somewhere above his actual eyebrows. He uses black eyeliner around his eyes, adding a little vertical line at the top and bottom of each. "These will make the eyes seem wider," he says. "And now the lips." He draws around them, exaggerating the curves of the upper lip, drawing the edges up into a smile. With a tube of lipstick, he applies red inside the line.

I remember Mama painting her mouth red just as Cosmo is doing, painting it red and then seeing how it stretched in a wide smile, checking the mirror to see if any of the red had escaped onto her teeth. "Me, too," I would beg, and she would paint my lips carefully, saying, "There you are, my little movie star."

Cosmo gestures at someone working in the lighting booth, and the room darkens, with just a spotlight on his face. Music comes softly through the sound system. A violin, I think, quiet, drifting music that seems to follow Cosmo around the stage as he strikes different poses. At one point, out of nowhere, he plucks a red flower and holds it as if it were the most precious thing in the world. And then it's gone, and a wash of sadness comes over the white face. The clown figure collapses, and the spotlight vanishes.

When it comes on again, he is behind Nathan, and the rest of us watch as Cosmo wipes his finger through the white of his cheek and uses the greasepaint to make a mark on Nathan's cheek. He does it to each of us in turn. Livvy has crept into the circle, and he puts a little streak of white on her face, too.

"The touch of the clown," Cosmo says in a voice so soft it is almost a whisper. "We pass it on from one to another. It was given to me by my clown-master. A little smudge of Clown White. It enters our pores and we are changed forever. We see the world in a different way. People see us in a different way."

And then he very carefully re-packs his make-up kit and closes the lid. With the spotlight still following him, he gives a little wave and exits. The lights in the theater come up.

For a couple of seconds everything is quiet, and then everybody begins talking at once, gathering up backpacks, heading out. Nathan comes over where Livvy and I are getting our things together.

"N-Nothing new for me," he grins. "My ancestors have been painting their f-faces for centuries."

"I'm going to be a clown, too," says Livvy, touching the greasepaint on her face.

"On you," I tell her, "it's more like Nathan's ancestors. War paint."

CHAPTER TEN

N athan walks us part way home. He likes to take different buses sometimes, he says, and he can catch one on 107th Avenue that will take him to the west end. He plays a game of tag with Livvy for a couple of blocks, both of them running circles around me, in and out of parking lots, darting into alleys, until Livvy begins to get tired.

"I don't want to walk anymore," she announces.

"Well, you have to. We still have eleven blocks to go."

She scowls at me and straggles half a block behind, dragging her feet. Nathan and I walk slowly on ahead.

"You're younger than everyone else in the workshop," he says. "Cosmo a friend of yours? Is that how you got in?"

"Just someone we happened to run into. Or rather, he ran into us." I tell Nathan about the accident. "But, yeah, he kind of snuck me in.

I'm almost fourteen. Cosmo says I look sixteen, though. How'd you get in?"

"Oh, you know. Counselor at school thought I was a hotshot in drama. T-Trying to get me away from bad influences."

"Bad influences?"

"Yeah. Th-The usual. You know, Mom and her b-boyfriend and my older b-brother all on booze. They think I'm next. Probably right." He has a nervous little laugh. "Y-You keep an eye on your little sister all the time?"

"Livvy? Yeah, I don't mind. Dad and Grandma aren't very…capable."

He looks at me quizzically. "C-Capable?"

What can I say? My dad's between jobs. He has health problems. Grandma is eighty-two and quite crippled.

I decide to be honest with him. "On the booze, as you say."

"Hey, we should introduce our families to each other. They c-could have one hell of a party."

We check to see if Livvy is still behind us. She turns her back when she notices us waiting for her.

"Don't pay her any attention. She just wants

us to go back and coax her along." Instead, we walk on even slower, stopping and looking in shop windows, but not really seeing what's in them except for the imperfect reflection of ourselves, side by side.

"Do you think it's true?" I look at Nathan. He's rubbing at the bit of greasepaint on his cheek.

"What?"

"That Cosmo has AIDS?"

"Yeah, it's true." Nathan is close enough that I can feel his hand brush against mine. "My uncle had it, too. He had KS."

"KS?"

"Some kind of skin cancer people with AIDS get. Cosmo has KS. You can see it on his arms. It looks just like my uncle's."

"Does that mean he's going to die?"

"I think people with AIDS are living longer all the time. Who knows, maybe someone will come up with a cure next week."

"How long did your uncle have it?"

"About ten years, I think. It was only the last c-couple of years he was really sick. My m-mom was kind of crazy. Wouldn't let me or my brothers go and visit him, but we'd sneak in and see him anyway. I liked my uncle. He was really f-funny."

Livvy has caught up with us. "I want an ice cream," she says, eyeing the store coming up on the next corner.

"Sorry," I say. "No money."

"Guess what?" Nathan says. "I've got just enough for three ice-cream cones and one pack of cigarettes. All the things we could need in life."

We sit on the bus bench and lick our cones. Nathan lets one of his buses go by before we finish. "There'll be another one along in a minute," he says, gesturing for us to continue the trek home. "Even f-faster if I light up a cigarette."

Livvy turns and waves at him every few steps until we can no longer see him. By the way she is walking, I can see she's had an accident, and I have to take her into the bathroom in a laundromat to change her back into the clothes that have blue paint spilled on them.

"I don't want to put these on," Livvy sobs.

"It's just for a little way."

She's still crying when we get to our block. "I hate these," she wails, dabbing her fingers into the blotches of blue on her shorts.

"When we get home," I say, "you can get out of these right away. And then, then..." I drag the word out, trying to think of something that will make her stop crying, "then we can do your most favorite thing to do. We can play jacks with Bingo, or we can color in your Pocahontas coloring book, or I can read to you out of *Winnie-the-Pooh*, or we..."

"Can we make something special to eat? Can we make brown sugar and banana sandwiches and color in Pocahontas, too?"

"If that's what you want."

Daddy hears us come in. "Where have you kids been?" he calls from the living room.

"Just to the library," I say, giving Livvy a little push up the stairs.

◆

A thunderstorm rolls in after the heat of the day. Great waves of sound rumbling across the sky, and sheets of light.

"You're supposed to unplug the TV in electrical storms," I tell Daddy and Grandma.

"We'll live dangerously," Daddy says, slipping a cassette into the VCR. "You kids want to watch this before you go to bed?"

The movie is called *Sarah Plain and Tall*. I know the story from a book I got in the library when I was in grade four. It is about a family in pioneer days, and the dad is raising his two children after his wife dies. He decides they need a mother so he advertises for one.

"Who's in this one?" Grandma asks. She's lost her cigarettes and searches for them as much as she can without getting out of her armchair, her hands checking through the mound of dishes and potato chip packages and tissues that have accumulated on her TV tray, patting the pockets of her housecoat, reaching toward the carpet.

"Glenn Close," Daddy says.

"Never heard of her." Grandma sounds disappointed. "She must be a new one. Livvy, be an angel and see if you can find my cigarette package. Claudette Colbert. People used to say I looked like her. I never saw it myself, but I did used to do my eyebrows long and thin with eyebrow pencil."

Livvy has found the cigarettes. "I want one," she says.

"Lord have mercy," Grandma cackles. "Where did you ever get such an idea? You give those over now, and you can have some of that apple cider Mrs. Perth brought when she came by today."

"She's not supposed to have sweet drinks before she goes to bed," I say.

Grandma fumbles with her lighter and finally gets her cigarette lit. Then she levels a gaze at me. Sometimes her eyes seem to be covered with fog, but not tonight. "I don't know what we'd do without you, Barbara," she says, as if she were cutting each of the words out with a pair of sharp scissors. "A little bit of apple cider isn't going to hurt this child."

"Yummee!" Livvy dances around with her drink, slopping it onto the rug.

Daddy is rolling his eyes to the ceiling. He doesn't like it when people talk during the movies. "You want to talk, I'll put it on Pause," he always says. He puts it on Pause now. "Can I pour you a little something, Ma?"

"I don't mind," Grandma says.

With juice glasses of sherry poured for himself and Grandma, and warnings about no more talking, he starts the movie again.

Glenn Close is too beautiful to be Sarah Plain and Tall, but I let myself sink into the movie. I wonder if people nowadays still send away for mail-order brides. What would happen if Daddy got a wife, a mother for Livvy and me? Would anyone marry someone Daddy's size? Maybe he would diet and quit drinking.

It isn't long before both Grandma and Livvy have fallen asleep. Daddy winks at me. In the old photographs with Mama, he is a good-looking man, overweight even then, but with dark wavy hair and a moustache. I think of him and Mama holding hands at the movie theater where they worked. And I can feel again the feeling, like the little spark of electricity that went running up my arm and then went racing around my body when Nathan's fingers kept brushing against mine as we were walking home. Different than the touch of Cosmo's fingers, so smooth with white grease-paint. Cosmo said it was a touch connecting us to the world of the clown.

In the world of *Sarah Plain and Tall*, the pioneer family gathers by a pond for a picnic. Green meadows stretch as far as you can see. The whole world seems to be made out of grass and sky. The little boy plays a harmonica. His sister has her sketchbook open. The father and Sarah joke shyly with one another. The dog runs back and forth over the picnic lunch and everyone yells at him and laughs.

This must be their perfect time. Hang onto it, Cosmo would say. Make a life preserver.

CHAPTER ELEVEN

n Wednesday when we get home, Daddy is watching for us at the door.

"I don't know why you kids can't stick closer to home," he says, eyeing the rolled-up piece of paper Livvy has squashed flat on the way home from the art gallery. "You're always wanting to go somewhere. And guess what—we are." He is trying to keep back a smile. I can see the edges of his lips quivering.

"Where? Where?" Livvy has forgotten how tired she is from the walk home and is dancing from foot to foot.

"Guess," Daddy says.

"Disneyland!" Livvy shrieks. "I want to go to Disneyland and see Pocahontas."

"Well, it's not quite Disneyland." Daddy laughs a thin laugh. "Mayfair Park. What do you think of that? Myron Perth is home for a couple of days and wants to take Mrs. Perth on a little outing tomorrow and said for us all to come along."

I feel like someone has opened a trap door and I am falling, without warning, everything gone from under my feet.

"How long will we be gone?" My voice comes out as a little squeak. "I mean, when will we be going? And coming back?"

Daddy looks at me sideways. "I don't know. Around noon, I guess. We can have lunch down there. Why are you interested in time all of a sudden?"

"Oh, no reason. Just wondered."

"Well, it doesn't really matter, does it?" Daddy backs toward the sofa. "It's summer holidays. If we're late it won't be like you have to get up and go to school the next day."

"Goodee." Livvy is jumping like a kangaroo around the living room. "We get to go to the park," she chants, tossing her flattened paper into a corner, just missing Grandma's ashtray. "Does it have a playground with a curly slide?"

"It has a gigantic playground." Daddy sinks back into his sofa. He is looking at me, waiting for me to be happy and excited. "I said we'd bring the hot dogs. You don't mind nipping down to the store, do you, hon? We got enough for weenies and buns but not a cab. Maybe

Livvy'll go along and keep you company."

"Me tired. Don't want to walk," Livvy whines.

"It's okay. I'll go," I say. "I don't mind."

"Get me some cigarettes, Barbara." Grandma's walker squeaks through the kitchen doorway. "I'm getting low."

The feeling is still in my stomach as I head for Cosmo's apartment. With everything inside me fallen, my feet move heavily up the steps to the landing. When I knock, there is no answer. As I begin to go back down the stairs, though, I see him coming down the street, moving lazily along on Mehitabel, singing as he goes. As he reaches the gate, he finishes the song—a little whispery song about an octopus's garden in the sea.

"Barbara." His eyes widen with surprise. "Didn't expect to find you on my doorstep. Something the matter?"

"Tomorrow..." I start to tell him and then my voice stops and won't go on.

"Hey, catch your breath." He gestures toward the bench by the patio table. "Close your eyes and relax a minute."

I close my eyes and spots dance around in the

sudden black. The air in my chest seems to be beating its way upward and I shudder.

"Okay?" I feel Cosmo's long fingers on my arm.

"Tomorrow's ruined. I can't come tomorrow."

"Hey." Cosmo's fingers slip down into my hand. "It's okay. It's not a problem. You want to tell me about it?"

"Daddy wants us to go to Mayfair Park with Mrs. Perth's son. I don't want to go, but if I say so, I know it'll hurt Daddy's feelings. We don't go…" I try to think how to finish the sentence. "Many places."

"You should then, and enjoy the park. You shouldn't even think about the workshop." Cosmo is busy putting Mehitabel into the shed. "Hey," he hollers from across the yard, "I got paid today. And whenever I get paid I feel it is obligatory to splurge on a triple cappuccino at the Italian center. So, Miss Barbara…" As he comes back across the yard, his voice thickens with a silly accent and he rolls his eyes at me. "I'ma aska you to be my date for da cappuccino. Whaddya say, kid?"

I nod. I may even be smiling. I can buy the hot dogs on the way home.

We sit at a little table in a corner. "Now isn't this like the movies," Cosmo chuckles. "We just need the gypsy with his violin." He says I have to order something, so I go for a large hot chocolate with whipped cream. When the brimming cups are brought to our table, the air is filled with the smells of chocolate and coffee and cinnamon from the sprinkles on top of his cappuccino.

"This is what makes life worth living," Cosmo says, nibbling on the foam. He senses my stricken look. "This is one of the things that makes life worth living," he corrects himself. "There are so many." But his voice sounds tired. "So you don't get to go out very much with your dad?" He licks the milk moustache off his upper lip.

"He's not well…not very well, and Livvy…"

"What exactly is Livvy's problem?"

"Well, you know…" I am surprised we are talking suddenly about Livvy. Cosmo can juggle topics, too. "She doesn't always get to the bathroom on time."

"Lots of little kids don't."

"But it's worse with Livvy. She's only got one kidney and sometimes she has even more than one accident in a day."

"And you clean her up."

"Most of the time."

We drink our drinks quietly for a few minutes, listening to the sound of the late-afternoon traffic getting all mixed up with Italian conversations at the tables around us.

"Daddy thinks it's because he and Mama were old when Livvy was born. I heard him telling Grandma, and then he cried. Mama was forty-four. Do you think that could be the reason?"

"I don't know." Cosmo holds his cappuccino cup in both hands. "Whatever the reasons, though," he moves his cup slightly forward like a kind of pantomime toast I've seen him do in skits at the workshop, "I think you're…" He looks around the room as if there is a word somewhere, and then he smiles. "I think you're swell." He is laughing, and I'm afraid he is going to choke on his cappuccino. "I can't believe I said swell," he says. "Swell. Some words should never be used. What I meant to articulate, Miss Barbara Stanwyck Kobleimer, is that I think you are caring and tenacious and talented."

"I don't mind swell," I say.

◆

Myron Perth drives a potato-chip truck. It says *Crispy Dan the Potato Chip Man* in big red letters on the outside.

"That's me," Myron Perth says. "I'm Crispy Dan. My professional nom-day-ploom." He wiggles his false teeth at Livvy and makes her laugh.

There is only room in the cab for two other people, Grandma and Mrs. Perth, but Crispy Dan has put a kitchen chair in the back of the panel for Daddy to sit on, and a foam mattress for Livvy and me.

"I'm gonna have to lock the back so you don't all fall out," Crispy Dan says, "so I'm assignin' you, Livya, to be the keeper of the light so none of them groblems get ya." Myron Perth talks like he has a mouth full of rags. He gives Livvy a large flashlight.

"Yippee!" Livvy beams it to all the corners of the truck, flashing it back to the tower of trays filled with bags of potato chips and cheese puffs. "Me hungry," Livvy shouts. The flashlight scampers over a bag of picnic stuff, and the woven plastic and metal pipes of folded-up lawn chairs.

"Keep that light in one place," Daddy says, settling onto the chair. "When you flash it all around it gives me motion sickness."

"Help yusself," Crispy Dan says before he bolts the door. "You girls each grab a bag to munch on. There's salt and vinegar on top, and ketchup on that second tray or, if you like dill pickle, there's a few left on that flat over there. You wan' one, Edwin, help yusself."

We hear the catch closing on the outside. Livvy clicks off the flashlight and we are all sitting in a thick, close blackness.

"Quit horsing around, Olivia." Daddy's voice cuts through the darkness. "If I'd known how primitive..." he mutters. "Olivia, turn that light on now and leave it on."

Livvy turns it on, beaming it onto my face, blinding me.

"Brat." I close my eyes. I wonder what they are doing at the clown workshop. I can imagine Cosmo on the stage with everyone gathered on the closest seat-steps surrounding it. In his soft voice he would be telling them things about what a clown does. I wonder where Nathan is sitting. I wonder if he's wondering where I am today.

"I want dill pickle," Livvy says. She gets up off the foam mattress, staggering back and forth in a mock effort to keep her balance. The light flashes all over the place. Daddy groans in his chair. "Can I have a beer?" Livvy says, stumbling over a case.

"Livvy, I'm beginning to lose my patience," Daddy says. "Sitting back here is intolerable," he mutters. Intolerable, I decide, is a good word to know. I say it twice, quietly.

At the campground, Daddy and Crispy Dan set up the lawn chairs for Grandma and Mrs. Perth. Livvy loves Crispy Dan. She follows him around. "You 'n' me," he says, "we better fine some kinling wood and get us-selves a good weenie fire goin' here, eh, Livya? Whaddaya think?"

"You want to walk down by the river," Daddy asks me, "while Myron and Olivia are looking for firewood?"

I'm surprised. My head nods automatically. We have walked only part of the way when I hear his breath coming out in wheezes. We walk slower. The path along the river is thick with trees, and it is cool with the sunlight blocked by branches.

"So quiet and peaceful," Daddy says, stopping and leaning with his hand at arm's length against a large poplar. "Whew. Am I out of shape."

"It's nice down here." I smile at Daddy. I can't think any more about the workshop. I look at Daddy, streams of perspiration running along his face. He finds a handkerchief and rubs it away, mussing his hair where it is turning gray at the edges. He pats it smooth again.

"Your mama and I used to go on picnics when we first got married," he says. "Uncle Potts—do you remember Uncle Potts and Auntie Vitaline? No. I guess not. You'd be only about two when they passed on. Always had a cottage at Alberta Beach for the summer, Uncle Potts and Auntie."

We have moved on to the edge of the river bank where we can look down and see the North Saskatchewan. It is low and muddy, moving with a summer slowness.

My mind is filled with questions. Was that the cottage we used to stay in at Alberta Beach? Why don't we have it anymore? Did you and Mama come to this park?

But before I can decide which question to ask first, Olivia and Crispy Dan burst through the bushes.

"Dad-dee," Livvy shrieks, "we got weenie roasting sticks and we can use them for marshmallows, too. And Uncle Crispy and I got goodles of wood, didn't we, Uncle?"

"Nuff to cook a moose," Crispy Dan says. "Boy, you gotta keep hoppin' to keep up to this 'un, lemme tellya. You never move' this quick, Eddie, I remember. We allus had to wait for you. You wuz the cow's tail."

"Cow's tail," Livvy giggles. "Daddy's the cow's tail."

"Oh, yeah," Daddy says. "This cow's tail could beat you any day, Miss Smartypants."

"No, no," Livvy shrieks, jumping up and down, and suddenly Daddy is stumbling up the path, weaving back and forth, making it impossible for anyone to get past him, but Livvy darts into the trees and comes out ahead of him. She is shrieking and laughing, her feet barely touching the ground, dancing back and forth in front of us all the way to the picnic tables.

"Lord have mercy," Grandma Kobleimer says. "What a ruckus. We could hear you coming half a mile away." She and Mrs. Perth are sipping from big glasses of pink Kool-aid.

"I want Kool-aid," Livvy says. "Me thirsty."

"How about you, Edwin?" says Crispy Dan. "We have kiddie Kool-aid, and..." he pulls out a big bottle of vodka that has been hiding inside the picnic bag, "we got the grownup version."

Livvy and I walk to the playground after we've stuffed ourselves with hot dogs. I take the survival bag with me, and when Livvy gets tired of playing on the equipment, we sit leaning against a big tire. Livvy draws a picture of a tiger roasting a marshmallow while I try to read. She talks nonstop, though, as she colors, and I give up on *Jane Eyre* and pull out the word-search book. There is one puzzle left. I work at it slowly to make it last as long as possible.

"Can we come here tomorrow?" Livvy asks. "I want to come here every day."

"What about art school? Don't you want to go anymore? Besides, we can't come tomorrow. This is a one-time thing."

"Oh, baa," Livvy scowls as she colors her tiger chartreuse with magenta stripes.

"Tigers are orange and black," I say.

"Not this one." Livvy looks at me defiantly.

I am searching for the word *pomegranate* in the puzzle book. It's a tricky puzzle filled with words that have a lot of p's in them: *hippopotamus, proposition, pepper*.

It is late in the afternoon when Livvy and I

walk back around the little lake to the picnic site. Before we can get to the shelter and picnic tables, we can hear Crispy Dan whooping with laughter.

"O-oh," he says when we get there, "betta not tell ya the enda that 'un. Little pitchers got bigyears." His words are even fuzzier, and Grandma and Mrs. Perth in their lawn chairs laugh at the way he staggers back and forth in front of the camp stove and makes funny faces at them. The vodka bottle hidden behind the picnic bag is nearly empty.

"Uncle Crispy's walking funny!" Livvy claps her hands. "I want to walk funny, too."

"Now see what you've done, Myron," Mrs. Perth cackles. "There'll be no stopping her now."

But Livvy does wind down. "Me want hot dogs," she says when it's past suppertime and Crispy Dan has brought out a few more bags of potato chips.

"There are no more. We ate them all at lunch."

"Pooh." Livvy makes a little hill of ripple-chip crumbs and starts dropping them into her grape Kool-aid.

"Smarten up." I grab the bag of chips away from her but she lets out one of her full-force shrieks.

"Barbara, you quit teasing the baby," Grandma hollers.

I give Livvy back her bag of chips but she bats it onto the ground.

"Be a brat. I don't care."

I go for a little walk around the campsite and expect she'll be tagging along in a minute or two. She doesn't, though, and when I get back, I see she has draped herself across the picnic table. I wish we were at home so I could get her to bed.

"Are you having a nap?" I ask her, but she just makes a cranky *mmm* sound for an answer. She doesn't want to hear *Winnie-the-Pooh* or draw pictures in the scrapbook or play catch with Bingo. The back of Crispy Dan's panel is open and I can see the end of the foam mattress.

"Let's play Pocahontas," I say. "In the tent of Pocahontas, her bed of soft buffalo-skins waits, ready for Pocahontas to lie down, to sleep and dream…"

"I'm not tired," Livvy grumbles. "I want to go in a canoe."

"Dream of the sky people who will come and

get her so she can go hunting with them, hunting through the stars, shooting arrows at the moon…"

"That's not in Pocahontas."

The vodka bottle is empty now and the grown-ups are drinking beer out of their Kool-aid glasses.

"What I wanna know…" Crispy Dan is waving his glass, flinging out splashes of beer and foam, "is why the guvment don't do nothin' for us. I mean, I should be legible…ellgible…illegible for disability…"

"Don't be hollering." Mrs. Perth looks like she's trying to get out of her lawn chair but can't quite do it. "Keep your voice down, Myron, or the cops'll be over here like a duck on a June bug."

A family at the next picnic site is quickly packing up their supper. They look over at us and the mother shakes her head back and forth with a sad look on her face.

"What's she staring at?" Daddy mutters and then says in a loud voice, "This is a public place…"

"Yes, it is a public place," the woman says, herding a couple of wide-eyed children Livvy's age into the back of the car.

Finally, after a trip to the washrooms in the shelter, I lure Livvy into the back of the panel and get her to lie down on the mattress. She curls herself into a ball and falls asleep almost at once. I turn on the flashlight and aim the beam at the page where I've left off in *Jane Eyre*.

Crispy Dan and Daddy are having an argument.

"Yeah, Edwin, tell someone who cares…" Crispy Dan chants over and over again. "The guvment don't care…"

I switch off the light and curl against Livvy. I can feel the tangle of her hair against my cheek. She makes little stirring sounds like a sleeping puppy. I fall asleep, too, until I feel the back of the panel shuddering as Daddy tries to climb in. It is totally dark now and he trips, falling into the trays of potato chips. The whole back part of the truck is filled with the sound of crashing trays and broken bags of chips being crunched by Daddy's flailing body. There is swearing and Livvy is suddenly wide awake and crying.

"What in tunnation goin' on?" Crispy Dan yells from the parking gravel below us. "Careful them trays. That's produce, y'know."

I can see Daddy lying on the floor of the truck when I finally find the flashlight. He is moaning. Crispy Dan slams the door shut and locks it.

"I don't like it in here," Livvy is screaming. "I want out." I try to wrap my arms around her. "No," she wails. "Let me go. I want out of here."

"Shhh," I say. "Everything's okay." When Livvy quits crying long enough to catch her breath, I realize that Daddy isn't making any sound at all. Maybe he's dead. Maybe he hit his head as he fell. The thought feels like ice when you hold it and it gets to be more than your skin can bear. I shine the flashlight back over him. He does look dead, a dead man with potato chips caught in his hair. And then I see his chest rise, and before Livvy can start into her crying again, I hear a snore against the sound of the truck motor.

The truck seems to go back and forth a lot on the road. More than once we can hear the sound of someone honking his horn loudly at Crispy Dan. Livvy's crying has settled into a quiet shuddering. Finally the truck gears down and, climbing up onto a curb, stops. I have kept the light on all the time and the beam finds Crispy Dan's face as he unbolts the door. He opens his mouth in horror at what has happened to the back of the truck and his trays of potato chips. "Awww…" It sounds like he's going to cry, and in the big circle of his mouth, I can see he has lost his teeth. "Get outta there you sumbitch," he hollers at Daddy and tries to climb up into the truck, but he slips and falls back, and lies gasping on the boulevard.

"Daddy." I let go of Livvy for a minute and shake his arm, but I know I won't be able to wake him. "C'mon, Livvy, we'd better get Grandma."

Livvy doesn't say anything. She is shuddering so that it seems she will never stop. I get her into the house and tell her to lie on the sofa while I get Grandma's walker back out to the truck. Mrs. Perth is fast asleep in the truck cab. For a minute, as she struggles to get down, it seems like Grandma is going to collapse, too. If she does, it will look like something has come and killed everyone in their tracks, a terrible plague with instant, deadly power—like the green smog that drifted through the palaces of the Egyptians in that movie about Moses that Grandma and Daddy often watch.

But Grandma's hands curl around the piping of her walker, and I am able to get her slowly into the house. I help her into her chair. Livvy is asleep now on the sofa. I get a blanket off Daddy's bed and take it out to the truck, brush the potato chips out of his hair and put it over him. Somehow Crispy Dan and Mrs. Perth have managed to get across the road to Mrs. Perth's house.

When I look out my bedroom window, I can see the panel truck sitting at its odd angle, half on the road, half on the boulevard. Maybe sometime I'll be able to tell Cosmo about this day. We'll sit in a coffee shop with cups of cocoa and cappuccino in front of us, and laugh at Daddy with his crown of potato chips. But for now, I want to push it out of sight, forget it.

"Tomorrow," the beautiful girl in *Gone With the Wind* is always saying. "Tomorrow."

Tomorrow I will be back in the workshop again.

CHAPTER TWELVE

Each day we seem to be getting faster at walking the fifteen blocks downtown. Today we are a quarter of an hour early. Livvy has been grumpy ever since she woke up, close to noon.

"Do you want me to go in with you?" I ask her when we get to the art gallery.

"No. I can go in by myself." She's already pulling the heavy outer door open.

"See you at break."

Nathan is sitting at a picnic table in the park, smoking a cigarette.

He waves at me.

"H-Hey, we missed you yesterday. C-Cosmo said you went on an ou-t-ting with your family."

I nod.

"A good t-time?"

I shake my head. "Mayfair Park with Crispy Dan the Potato Chip Man."

"You're k-kidding."

"It was okay to start with, but it went on forever, and everyone got plastered except Livvy and me."

"Everybody's idea of a p-picnic ain't the same, I guess." Nathan chuckles softly.

"You get home okay when we left you at the bus stop?"

"Oh, yes." Nathan does a little dance with his eyebrows. "B-But it didn't make any difference. No one else showed up. It was k-kinda nice having the house all to myself. Except I didn't know where anyone was, and when everyone d-did come crashing in, it was three o'clock in the morning, and my cousin passed out on my bed, leaving approximately thirty centimeters for me."

"Were you able to get back to sleep?"

"T-Took awhile. I ended up reading for about an hour."

"No kidding," I say. "I read to put myself to sleep, too. *Jane Eyre*, this book Cosmo gave me—it's good for that."

The noon sun finds touches of redness in Nathan's hair and face. He holds his nicotine-stained fingers over his chin to cover a new pimple that has a redness all its own.

"Wonder what Mr. Cosmo Clown has lined

up for us t-today?" He draws in smoke, hanging onto it inside for so long I think it must have seeped into all the corners of his body.

"You should try to quit smoking," I say, feeling my own face turn red. I hear Grandma's voice, thick with sarcasm. "Barbara, I don't know what we'd do without you."

"Just one of my bad h-habits," Nathan smiles.

"Tell us about the other ones." Cloud drops her backpack on the picnic table. She pantomimes lighting a cigarette and gestures at Nathan's pack. Nathan pushes it over to her.

"You wouldn't want to know."

Cloud launches into a replay of her morning with her mother. "I finally told her that if she signed me up for anything more this summer I'd run away and live with Daddy and spend the rest of the holidays lying in the sun getting sunburnt, eating junk food and getting fat. That nearly gave her cardiac arrest. Don't you hate it when parents try to just totally run your life?"

Nathan and I share a look.

I try to imagine Cloud and her mother in the morning, arguing over orange juice in crystal glasses on a table with a checkered tablecloth in one of those kitchens with islands of appliances and copper pots and jelly molds on the wall, like in the housekeeping magazines at school.

"It's my life, after all," Cloud continues as we head over to the theater. "I told her she should check to see if they were offering any summer courses on how to parent."

We are inside for only a few minutes today as Cosmo tells us about our assignment before leading us out onto the street. We are supposed to create characters that will be out of place in different spots downtown.

In a grungy alley, we are high society people; by an exercise gym, we are couch potatoes barely able to move; in a posh shopping district, we are street people.

"Don't need to pretend for this," Nathan whispers to me.

Cosmo is having a great time. He seems to bound with energy, gathering us to him wherever there's a parking lot or a small park. "Your greatest source of material," he tells us, "is the world around you. Did you notice the little boy, determined not to go a step farther with his mother on their shopping expedition? The little old lady in her Sunday hat, passing out leaflets?

Or the tattooed biker with the parking ticket on his motorcycle?" Suddenly Cosmo looks at his watch. "Oops," he says, "we'd better be getting back or Miss Olivia will be wondering what's happened to us."

It is five minutes until her class lets out.

"We'll go ahead." Nathan grabs my hand and we jog along the sidewalk back to the theater.

"Livvy," I call as we head back inside, "we're back." There is no answer. I have a feeling inside of me that something has gone wrong, a kind of empty feeling except for my heart pounding. A car screeches and slams on its brakes as I race across the street to the art gallery workshop. Everyone is gone from Livvy's class except for a strange woman rolling up papers.

"Livvy!" I call.

"I think everyone's gone," the lady says, snapping a rubber band around the papers.

"But Livvy waits with me."

"Oh. The little girl with a…bathroom problem. She said she had to go and see you about half an hour ago. She said her sister's across the road."

"Where's Bella?"

"She was sick. Couldn't make it in today.

Didn't your sister find you? I thought she knew just where to go."

"Oh, God." I hear my voice coming out, a little moan, the sound finding its way past the dryness in my mouth, my throat.

"Isn't she h-here?" says Nathan.

"I think she's gone home."

I'm out on the street again, running, Nathan just behind me. "Livvy," I cry. It seems to help to call her name as my feet fly over the cement. At the red lights I hop up and down.

"We'll catch up," Nathan says, his own breath coming in huffs and puffs. But we don't. She is nowhere along the fifteen blocks home. And then I am outside the house. The front door is open, like a rectangular scream, and the windows on either side seem to stare at me.

"Livvy," I shout, "are you home?"

It is Grandma who appears at the door, pushing her walker in front of her.

"Barbara Kobleimer," she shrieks, "you get in here. This instant!"

"Is Livvy..."

"She's inside," Grandma hollers. "And you better hightail it in here this instant." I see she is giving Nathan the once-over.

"You want me to w-wait?"

"No, you'd better get back to the class. Cosmo will be wondering what happened to us."

"Missy..." Grandma is still shrieking.

"Can I call you later?" Nathan positions himself in front of me, his back to Grandma.

"We don't have a phone."

"Well, let me give you my number. Maybe you can call me from a pay phone."

"Barbara!" Grandma is beside herself. I can hear her actually lifting her walker and slamming it down. Nathan searches for a slip of paper, pulls the flap off his cigarette box, finds the stub of a pencil in a pocket.

"Your father will hear about this!"

Nathan squeezes my hand, leaving the slip of paper. "I'll look after your bag," he says. "Call me." I watch him retreating down the block.

I tuck the paper in my pocket and head for the door. I have to squeeze past Grandma's walker.

"You deceitful girl." Her words seem to be hurled at me. "You can thank your lucky stars that Livvy got home by herself. Lord only knows what might have happened to her..."

"Where is she?"

"Her daddy is attending to her upstairs."

As I make my way up the stairs, I can hear Livvy's muffled sobs. The door to her room is open and she spies me as Daddy pulls a clean T-shirt over her head. She stares at me for a second.

"I couldn't find you." She is really crying now. "Where were you?" The words will hardly come out.

Daddy whirls around.

"The class was just out for a little while downtown. I didn't mean—" I'm not sure what I'm going to say, but I don't have a chance to say any more.

In three giant steps, Daddy has made it from Livvy's room and across the hall to the top of the stairway. He grabs my arm, pulling me away from the stairs. With his free hand, he slaps me across the face. I can hear the smacking sound and the pain bursts a second later. I think my head is going to fly away. He lets go of my arm and then the freed hand explodes against the other side of my face.

"Don't, Daddy!" My voice becomes a cry mixed with Livvy's shrieks.

With both hands, he grabs my shoulders and shakes me. I am screaming one big scream and the sound rattles around me. He lets go and I feel another slap against my cheek. There is a pause and then the other cheek, a horrible smashing into my eye.

"You think you can defy me." He is yelling at the top of his voice. I roll onto the floor and hold my hands over my head. The slaps stop but the voice rages on. "You think you can just go ahead and do what you damn well please whenever you damn well please. Well, not just yet, Miss Uppity. You're not of age, and until you are, you will do what I say. You hear? You hear? Answer me."

"I hear." I cry softly, not wanting to cry, my tears dampening the rag rug on the landing.

"I think you better apologize to your sister."

"I'm sorry, Livvy."

"Edwin." I can hear Grandma's quavery voice from the bottom of the stairs. "Son?"

"Yes, Mama."

"You come down and rest yourself before you have an attack."

"Rest! When do I ever get any rest with one child handicapped and the other a delinquent!"

"Edwin. Your blood pressure."

I am afraid to move. I can feel the rough surface of the rug against my stinging cheek, the smooth linoleum against my fingertips.

"You get to your room now, and don't come out." Daddy is still shouting.

"I want Barbara," Livvy howls.

"You leave her be," Grandma calls up. "She's been a deceitful, wicked girl."

"I want Barbara," Livvy is chanting as I get up and make my way past Daddy, standing there, his open hand shaking. I ease the door closed and then crawl onto my bed and hide my face in a pillow. A pain shoots along the inside of my ear. I am crying like Livvy cries, as if everything inside me is broken and will never get fixed. I cry until it seems like there is no more moisture in my body. In the quiet time that follows, I keep my eyes closed so that I am in a kind of velvet blackness, a cocoon of darkness.

CHAPTER THIRTEEN

I t is dark when I wake up. The ache in my ear is still there and my face feels hot and puffy. I ease myself off the bed and pull the light cord. For a minute, I'm afraid to look at myself in the little oval mirror on the wall across from my bed. I run a comb through my hair first, let the night air brush against my face from the window. The street is quiet. An old man walks a scruffy little dog, white with black spots. Under a streetlight, a woman with rhinestones on her shoes shifts from foot to foot, smoking a ciga-rette.

When I look at myself in the mirror, I see the sides of my face have begun to darken with bruises. In the movies, beaten women wear dark glasses. I will need to wear a sack over my head.

I wonder where everyone is. I can hear the hum of the refrigerator from downstairs, adding a kind of throb to the rise and fall of television talk. Where is Livvy?

She's asleeep in her room, curled into a quilt

162

on the floor, her thumb in her mouth, Bingo ball rolled off into a corner. She stirs as I watch her, and makes a little moan, like a kitten. I think of her trudging the fifteen blocks home from downtown, frightened, crying, her clothes soiled. In a way, my sore cheeks make it easier to think about this.

Downstairs, Daddy has fallen asleep, spilling the sherry that was left in his glass down his shirt. His mouth is open. When I look at his hands, resting palms up on the couch, I feel something hot and acidy rising inside me. For a minute I think I am going to throw up, but I close my eyes and it goes away.

Grandma is asleep in her chair, too. A cigarette on her ashtray has burned itself into a complete ash-ghost of itself. She snores softly, her head fallen to one side. On the TV, an old black-and-white movie flickers.

It is the Barbara Stanwyck movie about the *Titanic*. We watched it a couple of nights ago. I sit down for a minute on the edge of the sofa, very carefully so as not to wake anyone. The ship has already hit the iceberg and the captain is telling Barbara Stanwyck's husband, "I'm ordering all women and children into the boats."

"You look fat and funny in those lifejackets. Like Tweedledum and Tweedledee," the father says to his children. The night is riddled with the sound of foghorns, sirens wailing, the creaking of the lifeboats being lowered. A cute college boy, trying to disentangle the ropes, plunges into the sea and is pulled into the lifeboat. The *Titanic* sits in the still, black ocean, nosing slowly into the ice floes, and I think of the people moving up the great staircase and along the deck looking for lifeboats when there are no lifeboats left.

Maybe things could be worse than they are. I've lost Mama but children on the *Titanic* lost parents, and since then there have been wars, with children losing everything. I think of Jane Eyre, how things were so awful before she learned how to cope at the girls' school. The thing is to be strong and do what you have to do, to know what you have to do.

Right now I have to see Cosmo, no matter what Daddy has said about me leaving my room. And I should call Nathan. Maybe I will be able to call him from Cosmo's apartment, but if Cosmo isn't home I'll have to use a pay phone.

I ease Grandma's purse away from where it

rests on a TV tray by her ashtray. There's not much in it: a couple of bills, some dead lighters and a few coins. I take the quarters.

The clock on the funeral home shows that it's nearly nine-thirty. The light is on in Cosmo's living-room window, but when I tap on the door, there is no answer. I knock again and I'm almost ready to go back down the stairs when the door opens. Cosmo looks rumpled, as if he has just gotten out of bed. He is holding his sides and coughing, and he starts to smile at me but then he gasps.

"Barbara Stanwyck! Are you okay?"

All of the things I want to say stick in my throat, allowing only a great sob to get by, and I feel tears streaming down my face.

"Hey," Cosmo says, wrapping his arms around me. I can feel how thin he is, all the bones of his body, and his coughing begins again. Great racking coughs making a duet with my own sobs.

"Come in," he says. "We make quite a pair. Tell me what happened." He runs water into his little green tea kettle and puts it on the stove to heat.

My voice stops every few minutes for a sob

break as I tell him. I feel his thin, long hand against my shoulder, massaging the tightness. He removes it to stifle a cough.

"I stopped by your house," he says, "but your dad didn't want to talk to me, and he got quite angry when Livvy wanted to invite me in. Sent her upstairs and that made her cry again. I thought I was making matters worse so I left."

"It was all my fault," I say.

Cosmo has finished making tea. It smells like apples and cinnamon. He is very quiet as he swirls the brew in his cup, and his eyes are angry.

"Never think that," he says. "Unlucky things happen sometimes. It was unlucky that we were gone when Livvy came to find us." Some of the anger has left his eyes and he slumps in his chair as if he is very tired.

I sip the tea, the warmth seeping into me like a gentle wave.

"Barbara, I want to report what's happened here to the police. Do you know what I'm saying? You are a child. You and Livvy are children, and you're being robbed of something that's rightfully yours."

"Robbed?"

"Robbed of your chance to be a child. And

166

physically abused. No one has the right to hit you like that."

"But what will happen?"

"They'll likely take you and Livvy away and put you in a home where you won't have to worry about the things you've had to worry about. And Livvy will get some medical attention."

"Leave Daddy and Grandma?"

"It will be better."

"What if it isn't?"

"It has to be." A cough seizes him, dry and rattling something inside.

"The police for you; a doctor for me."

"A doctor?"

"I think my pneumonia's come back. Damn," he says. "And I was feeling so good earlier today. Must have overdone it. So, what do you say? I can pick up the phone right now."

"It's the first time he's hit me."

"He didn't hit you, Barbara. He beat you. I think the police might call it aggravated assault or something like that. They have big words for the bigger crimes. But we're also talking about neglect."

The tears stream off my face into the tea.

"I don't know what to do. What if Livvy and I are put in different places? I don't think Livvy could get along without me."

"I think they'd try to keep you together."

Cosmo is coughing again. "I'm going to have to get to the hospital," he says. "It's getting worse." He has come around behind me and I feel both of his hands on my shoulders. "I'm going to ask you to do something very brave. I'm going to ask you to see the police and tell them everything you've told me. Sometimes it's easier not to face things, and you've made it easy for your dad and your grandma not to face things. It's harder and braver to stare our demons in the eyes and say I'm not going to let you get me. I know, Barbara."

"Okay." My voice doesn't sound brave. It is hardly more than a whisper.

It doesn't take the police long to come. There are two of them. One for Grandma and one for Daddy, I wonder, or one for Livvy and one for me. Cosmo does most of the talking between bouts of coughing. But the older policeman asks me some questions and gets me to turn my face full toward Cosmo's kitchen light.

"I think we'll get both of you to the hospital.

I want a doctor's report on Barbara here, and you might as well come along if you need to get down there anyway."

It is a long night filled with questions and forms, and someone taking pictures of my face. "Here, kid, grab yourself a pop," the younger policeman says to me in the hospital waiting room. He gives me a dollar coin and gestures to a pop machine in the hall. Beside the machine there is a row of pay telephones. I fish one of Grandma's quarters out of my pocket along with the flap from Nathan's cigarette package, and dial the number.

"Yeah?" It's a woman's voice.

"Is Nathan there?"

"Na-than." I can hear party noise in the background. "Nathan, one of your girlfriends. You don't mind me sayin' that, do you? We jes like to tease little Nathan a bit."

"H-Hello."

"It's Barbara."

"Hey. Where are you?"

He listens while I go over, once again, the events of the afternoon and evening. I manage to do it without crying, although I have to pause and catch my breath a couple of times.

"I'm coming down," he says. "I'll bring your bag."

"I don't know how long I'll be here."

"See you in a few minutes."

I wonder how he'll get to the downtown emergency ward. The young policeman is watching me as I hang up the phone and get my can of pop.

"Calling home?"

"No. Just a friend."

"Constable Beauchamps and I'll be heading over to your house to talk to your dad, so it's probably a good idea not to call him."

"I won't."

When I am through seeing the doctor, Nathan is sitting in one of the mustard-colored vinyl chairs in the waiting room, with my survival bag beside him.

"I b-borrowed my friend's bike," he says.

Cosmo comes back into the waiting room and leaves some papers at one of the desks. "Hey, guy—good to see you," he says to Nathan, giving his shoulder a squeeze. "Looks like they're going to keep me here for awhile. Means I'm going to have to track down a friend of mine to take over the workshop for a few days. Maybe you can get back in, Barbara, once things settle down." The coughing seems to grab Cosmo and bend him in two. An orderly comes along with a wheelchair and Cosmo lowers himself into it.

"Keep an eye on this girl, Nathan," he says. He turns to me. "And you—just keep being as strong as you have been tonight, and do what's right for you and Livvy. I'll be thinking about you."

"I will, and you—" But the orderly is wheeling Cosmo away before I can finish.

It is close to one o'clock when Constable Beauchamps says we are finished. Nathan and I have practically fallen asleep over word-search puzzles, and the police offer to put his bike in the trunk of the cruiser and drop him off on our way. I am to be placed, at least temporarily, with a family on the south side.

"Will Livvy be coming, too?"

"If your dad and your gram are still passed out, most likely tonight. If they're...functional...we'll wait until tomorrow to sort it all out."

Nathan whispers to me, "Give me a call tomorrow," and squeezes my hand when the cruiser stops to let him out.

A full moon floats over the latticed steelwork

of the bridge spanning the river as we head to the south side. Somehow I feel as far away from myself as the moon.

Maybe this is what it is like to go beyond your death. I look down from the night sky and see a police car moving along the pavement ribboned with the yellow glow of streetlights, pulling into the driveway of a big, modern house in a subdivision. It is the only building in the crescent with its lights on.

My throat is dry and I feel an ache across my chest as we get out of the car. Someone is waiting at the door. We are halfway up the walk when I turn and dart back to the cruiser.

"Just a minute," I say. "I forgot my survival bag."

CHAPTER FOURTEEN

I am in a basement room with little windows high up in the wall. It is a room of white wicker and frilly, flowered cloth—the same cloth on the curtains and the bedspread and the cushions on the wicker chairs. On the walls there are pictures with wicker frames, and a mirror framed to match. There's a little wicker shelf crowded with tiny glass animals.

For a minute I think I must be dreaming. Then I remember. My face, when I look at it in the mirror, has puffed up even more, and one of my eyes is almost swollen shut. The other is red from crying, I guess, and reading late into the night. My survival bag is by the night table, where *Jane Eyre* lies turned over at the spot I left off.

Someone is hovering at the door.

"Are you awake, dear?"

It's Mrs. Hetherington. "Call me Auntie Sophie," she said last night.

"You were sleeping so soundly I didn't want to

wake you after all you went through yesterday. But I thought you'd like to know that Olivia is on her way over. She'll be here in a few minutes."

"Livvy?"

"Of course it may be just temporary, but Harold and I would be thrilled to have two little girls again. Our own, Luanne and Laverne, are grown up and moved away. This here was Luanne's room. Mind you, I've fixed it up a bit since Luanne left. She had pictures of that—who was it now?—Donny Osmond, I think, all over the walls. If you look you'll still see pinpricks where she tacked them, but you don't notice them too much with that small pattern on the wallpaper. That's her glass collection."

Auntie Sophie is not even as tall as I am. As she talks, she moves around the room, straightening the bottom of the bedspread, rearranging the little glass animals on the wicker shelf, adjusting the curtains, smoothing with her fingertips a couple of the pinpricks Luanne left in the wallpaper. Her smile is outlined in orange lipstick.

"Now, here I've been yammering on and you must be starved to death. Harold made up a pile of pancakes and sausages and there's still some in the oven. We ate hours ago. Harold—Uncle Hal—is an early riser even if he is semi-retired and only works afternoons now. Up at the crack of dawn. To tell you the truth, I wouldn't mind having a wee sleep-in once in awhile. Gracious, I think I hear a car now. It's either Harold back with the groceries, or else your sister. You get dressed and come right up, honey. Your little sister is going to want to see you're here, I'm sure."

Livvy has been crying, but she has been won over for the moment with an Oreo-cookie blizzard from the Dairy Queen, which she clutches in both hands. An ordinary man in a suit is with her. He is carrying a large cardboard box.

"You must be Barbara," he says. "I'm Jim Beresford. I've gathered together some of your things—and Olivia's."

"Barbara," Livvy squeals when she sees me. "Daddy's crying," she tells me in a rush, "and he says he's going to kill himself, and Grandma says they might as well kill her, too. Do you want some of my blizzard?"

"No. It's okay."

"Can we go home?"

"Oh, no, honey!" Auntie Sophie has a hold on Uncle Hal who has shown up with a bag of groceries in one hand. "You've only just got here, and we're going to have such a good time."

Uncle Hal says, "You come on in and see my model train set-up. Won a couple of prizes with it. If you're real careful you can look after the switch that makes them stop and go. Would you like that, Olivia?" Uncle Hal is a tall man with comfortable-looking wrinkles. He ends everything he says with a little snort of a laugh. "If you stay for awhile, you could even help me set up another track."

Jim Beresford tells the Hetheringtons that he'd like to have a word alone with me.

"Why, sure thing." Auntie Sophie ushers us into a den off the living room.

"I want to stay with Barbara." Livvy looks defiantly at the circle of grown-ups.

"Now, what about that train switch?" says Uncle Hal. "I was really hoping you could figure out how to make it go. It's tricky to keep an eye on everything and keep track of the switch, too."

"I can make it go." Livvy slurps the last of her blizzard with noisy, sucking sounds through her straw. She dances from foot to foot.

"You'd better go to the bathroom," I remind her.

176

"No, I don't need to. I'm going to see the trains."

With the door to the den closed, Jim Beresford takes a file out of a briefcase.

"How's your face?"

"Ugly."

"It'll look a lot better in a few days."

"How's Daddy?"

"I won't lie to you. He was pretty torn up. We're going to give him a chance to turn things around. He's agreed to go, for a month, to a treatment center for alcoholics. We tried to convince your grandma to go, too, but she wouldn't have anything to do with it so we'll have to put her into a nursing home for awhile. She's pretty run down, doesn't seem to have been eating properly for a long time. Won't acknowledge she has a drinking problem."

"Will we ever be back with Daddy?"

"It really depends on him. If the treatment program is successful..." As he talks, he writes things on forms from the folder. "I think he's truly sorry for what he did to you, but that doesn't make it okay, and there's been a lot of neglect. You'll find the Hetheringtons are very kind. They've taken in children before for the department."

"Do they know about...about Livvy's problem?"

Jim nods. "And, actually, Sophie worked as a registered nurse before she was married, so I think she can handle that. Olivia strikes me as the kind of youngster who has a lot of resilience. I think she'll fit in fine with the Hetheringtons.

"And me?"

Jim looks up from his forms. "You're more guarded," he says. "But you're used to accommodating people and I think that will help you through...this transition. I hope that, well, that you can quit being an adult for awhile and enjoy the Hetheringtons. They're dying to look after both of you, but that may be hard for you to accept when you've been doing all of the looking after on your own. Give it a try?"

I nod.

"Any questions?"

"There are people..."

"People?"

"Friends. Can I still see them?"

"Well, the Hetheringtons will be your guardians. But I can also act as something of a...liaison. Do you want me to contact them? Then, maybe I can arrange some way for you to be in touch with them."

"Yes," I nod again. "Please."

I tell him about Cosmo and Nathan, and he scribbles some notes into a little book he carries in his jacket pocket. "I want you to think of me as a friend, too," he says, leaving me a card with his name and phone number on it. "I spent a couple of years in a foster home when I was a teenager. It wasn't great. They put me in with a family that seemed okay on the outside but was having lots of problems when you closed the kitchen door. So it's important to me that I find good homes for young people in my charge." He has warm brown eyes and little lines of worry across his forehead. His fingers keep checking just above the worry lines, where there used to be hair.

When he opens the door to the den, Livvy is bouncing up and down, waiting for us.

"Barbara, I made the trains go and they went real fast and I thought there was going to be a crash, but Uncle Hal made it stop just before it happened. Right, Uncle Hal?"

"Righto, kid. You're a demon on that switch. Now let's go and see what damage we can do to that pile of flapjacks and sausages I was telling you about."

"Oh, goodee." Livvy flashes her dimples.

I know what Jim Beresford means.

•

It's only been a few days since I saw Jim Beresford, but I wish he would call. Is Cosmo out of the hospital yet? Nathan would know. I've tried phoning him twice but each time I get his mother. "You gotta be kidding. I'm the last person to know where he is," she says the second time I phone. "I'm just his mother."

It's hard to find a time when Auntie Sophie isn't watching me and I can get hold of the phone for a few minutes. How long does it take for a hospital to fix pneumonia? Maybe Cosmo is already at home resting. One of the times Livvy and I went over to Cosmo's apartment, I peeked in his bedroom as we headed back from the bathroom. His bed was filled with gigantic cushions covered in embroidery and patch-work—even, it seemed, bits of silver and gold and tiny odd-shaped mirrors. A bed out of *The Arabian Nights*. Maybe he's there now, on that ocean of cushions, sleeping, or reading, or listening to the lady with the sad, scrapy voice singing. *God Bless the Child*.

"Barbara." Livvy is calling me. I wonder if

she's had an accident. And then I remember she doesn't call me for that anymore. Not since Auntie Sophie's been looking after her.

I go to the bottom of the basement stairs. "What?"

"Guess what I'm doing?"

"Pretending you're a sweet little girl?"

"No. Guess."

"Don't know."

"Come up."

I climb the stairs but my legs feel so tired I can hardly do it.

"Making muffins." Livvy cackles. "Muffins. Muffins."

"Your face looks so much better today, Barbara." Auntie Sophie stops spooning muffin batter into a couple of pans she has waiting on the counter. Livvy is on a stool beside her, licking her fingers, chanting a song she has made up with lots of yummy-yummies in it.

I know what my face looks like. It still looks like I got hit by a truck. One eye is pretty well swollen shut. It's green and purple and blue all at once.

"I'm helping Auntie Sophie," Livvy chirps.

"She's such a dear." Auntie Sophie has a jar of

Smarties which she's shaking onto the top of the muffins. Livvy's hand darts out and she catches some. She giggles like a demented Munchkin.

"And I think we're just going to get on top of her health problems in no time. What this little girl needs is a good diet, and routine, and proper rest. When I think of what she's been through. Well." Auntie Sophie holds the Smarties jar in the air as if it were a weapon she'd like to use against Daddy and Grandma. Maybe me. "I suspect she got her kidney infection in the first place because of a lack of sanitation. Likely she was run-down. That's when nephritis strikes, when you're run-down, and those itty-bitty germs are just waiting to pounce..."

Keep talking, Auntie Sophie, I think. You know it all. When I close my eyes, I see the laundry sink in the basement with Livvy's clothes and bedding soaking. I smell the bleach. I think of the thousands of times I've helped her clean up and change.

"But all that's going to be different now, isn't it, lamb? Auntie Sophie's not going to let any of those nasty germs near..."

I try to block out the sound of the woman's words buzzing around the kitchen like a bunch of dizzy flies. I wish I had my word search but it's downstairs in the survival bag.

"And all that alcohol and smoke. Gracious heavens, I shudder to think what you've been through." Auntie Sophie is slipping the muffin pans into the oven and Livvy is licking the mixing bowl with big slurping noises, smacking her lips and burping.

"Quit acting dumb," I say to her, and she gives her tongue a rest from licking the bowl long enough to stick it out at me. Auntie Sophie almost catches her but Livvy gives her a sugary Shirley Temple smile.

"You were probably both born with fetal alcohol syndrome," Auntie Sophie says, closing the oven door and taking the mixing bowl from Livvy.

I know about fetal alcohol syndrome. The man from the alcohol and drug abuse center told us all about it in one of Ms. Billings' health classes. Expectant mothers who drink, giving birth to alcoholic babies.

Stop talking, I try to say, but Auntie Sophie's voice goes on and on, like the churning of the dishwasher. You don't know anything about Mama, so just shut up.

"It can lead to all kinds of psychological and physical problems." Her voice won't stop. Livvy has hopped down and is trying to see into the oven. "Hyper-activity, lack of attention…"

I feel each word pounding into me. My chair crashes to the floor and suddenly I'm running downstairs. I slam the bedroom door and turn the lock.

Someone is screaming. Someone is knocking Luanne's glass collection all over the room.

The someone is me.

It only lasts a minute and then I am on the floor, searching for the bits of glass. There is the head of the zebra. There is the glass whale. It's not broken at all.

A hand is banging on the door.

"Barbara!" Aunt Sophie shrieks. "Open this door! Open this door right away!"

Close to the ruffle on the bedspread, I can see a piece of the glass monkey. I crawl over and add it to the little pile.

"Baarbraa," Livvy is wailing.

I get up and unlock the door.

"Barbara, whatever's the matter?" Auntie Sophie nearly falls into the room. She gives her chest some little pats as if she's trying to get something that's stopped going again. Then she sees the pile of Luanne's glass pieces. She gasps and holds tight to the top of her dress. I watch as her mouth opens and closes like a goldfish that's flopped out of its bowl.

"Barbara." It is Livvy who finally speaks, choking my name out of the end of one of her sobs. "I want Daddy. I want to go home."

"I'm sorry." I'm not sure if Auntie Sophie hears me. "I'll buy some new ones for Luanne."

"I want to go home."

"Hush, sweetie." Auntie Sophie quits sputtering and pulls Livvy to her. "That was a very…hurtful thing to do." She looks at me in a way that makes me feel about the size of one of Luanne's glass animals. "She collected those for years."

"I'm sorry. I'll…"

"They can't be replaced."

Livvy spies the glass elephant over by the window and runs to pick it up.

"That's a good girl." Auntie Sophie's voice sounds like it might begin crying in a minute. "You help Barbara pick these up. I want to talk to Harold about this."

I'd better start packing. Not that I have much

with me to pack. Livvy has made a pile of glass fragments on the corner of Luanne's desk, and then she creeps out of the room and I hear her go upstairs.

Uncle Hal, when he comes down later, doesn't tell me to get my things together. He looks at the pile of glass pieces and picks a couple of them up.

"It's funny what people collect," he says. "Me and my trains. That was something I wanted to do when I was twelve but I never started doing anything about it until about ten years ago when the girls left home. Now, Luanne, I don't think she ever cared much about this collection. It was more her mother's idea. She got one little glass animal for her birthday one year. And then Sophie got it into her mind that Luanne was collecting them. After awhile, I think Luanne started believing it, too. But if it was something really dear to her, I think she would have taken it with her."

"I'm sorry," I mumble. "I didn't mean to smash them."

"Sophie said some things, didn't she?"

I look down at the carpet. There's a piece of glass we've missed, half hidden behind a leg of the wicker chair.

"Sometimes she doesn't think how things might sound." Uncle Hal's voice is very soft. "Now, let's just forget about this. It's over, and Sophie's feeling sorry, too. I'll ask Luanne if she'd like us to get new ones for her and, if she does, we'll work something out."

I don't start crying until Uncle Hal leaves the room. I hide my face in Luanne's flowery bedspread. When I look up, I see Livvy has crept back into the room.

"What do you want?"

"I'm sorry." Livvy's face crumples. "I won't lick the dish out noisy again."

"It's okay. I'm not mad at you. I just want to be alone for awhile. I've got a headache."

"When it's finished, will you read to me?"

"Sure," I say. I'm a better reader than Auntie Sophie. She gets half the names wrong in *Winnie-the-Pooh*.

◆

On the weekend, the Hetheringtons pack a picnic and take Livvy and me out to Alberta Beach for the day.

"I want you to tell me what you'd like to do, Barbara," Auntie Sophie had urged, watching as I finished a chapter of *Jane Eyre*, putting it down for a minute and stretching. "We've been doing all kinds of things for Livvy, you know, taking her out for pizza and to the park, and renting movies, but we haven't really done anything special just for you."

I think she and Uncle Hal have had a talk about me.

"I'm fine. I don't really feel like doing anything."

"Your face is looking ninety percent better. You could go out now and nobody would notice anything, I'm sure. You think of something you'd like to do this weekend. Your choice." Auntie Sophie can't be turned off once she's got an idea in her mind, so I told her about being at the beach with Mama, and how much I loved it. Almost wiggling with pleasure, she called Uncle Hal up from his trains and they worked out the details.

"Goodee, goodee. A picnic." Livvy bounces into the car, acting as if the whole thing is her idea.

"What have you got in the bag, honey?" Auntie Sophie asks me.

"Oh, just the stuff I always take with me."

"*Winnie-the-Pooh?*" Livvy asks.

"Of course."

"Read me some on the way out. I like the part about Piglet where he is entirely surrounded by water."

"Did you hear that, Harold?" Aunt Sophie says. "Livvy my love, you are developing an amazing vocabulary."

Astounding—she can remember a chapter heading, I think.

When we get there, the Hetheringtons find a picnic table close to the beach.

I want to find the spot where Mama and I used to spread our beach towels. "You want to do some word searches?" I ask Livvy.

"No. Uncle Hal and I are going to get double-dipped ice-cream cones."

"Well, whoop-dee-do," I say, but not loud enough for anyone to hear.

It takes a little while but I'm pretty sure I find our spot. I lie on the big striped towel Auntie Sophie has given me. I have sunscreen and word searches. Auntie Sophie refused to make dill-pickle sandwiches. She has her own ideas of a picnic lunch. Hot dogs with home-made relishes, simmered onions in a little thermos, enough potato salad to feed the town of Alberta Beach.

"Dill-pickle sandwiches!" She actually shuddered.

The beach is crowded—kids running back and forth squealing, adults baking themselves, some teenagers horsing around. Three old ladies in straw hats watch everything from a bench. There is the smell of the lake, a smell of dampness and dead fish, cut wood and evergreens. Gulls hover over the sand watching for food. Every now and then they drift back into the sky, their cries lost in jittery music from ghetto blasters.

I close my eyes, letting myself slip into the warmth and the smells and sounds. It seems as if Mama could be very close. "How's my big girl?" I think I hear someone say, but the words become caught on the squeal of a gull and carried away.

How you could fall asleep in the middle of so much activity, I don't know, but I think I do for a little while. Or maybe it's only a half-sleep and a half-dream with Nathan and Cosmo beside me. Nathan is handsome in his trunks, his skin like buttered toast. He smokes quietly, watching me, his hand moving toward me but not quite touching. "Cosmo," I say. "You should cover up." The lesions on his arms are on his chest and legs, too. "The sun can't be good for your skin."

"In a couple of minutes," he says, smiling at me. "I want to explore a little more of your perfect time." His green eyes wash over me, and then he sighs and the lids close, and he lies still with his arms folded over his thin chest, the ridges of his ribs.

A kid stumbles against me and jolts me back.

"Elvis, watch where you're going," a woman yells.

When I look around, Auntie Sophie waves at me from the picnic table where she sits crocheting in the shade. I turn to the last few pages of *Jane Eyre*. I read slowly, trying to make the book last, not wanting it to end.

Jane! Jane! Jane! a voice calls out.

The page seems hot enough to burn my fingertips.

…it was the voice of a human being—a known, loved, well-remembered voice…and it spoke in pain and woe, wildly, eerily, urgently.

"I am coming!"

Cosmo!

I grab the towel, *Jane Eyre* and my survival bag, and hurry over to the picnic table.

"Can we go?" I ask Auntie Sophie.

"Heavens! We've just got here. We haven't even had lunch."

"Can we eat now?"

"I thought you wanted to spend the whole day."

"I'm starved," I say, digging into the picnic hamper.

"You let me do that, honey." Sophie whisks her crocheting away into her sewing bag. "We'll just get these wieners on the go. Such a good idea, a picnic, and just a perfect day. Harold and I get to be such stick-in-the-muds when we're just by ourselves. Luanne and Laverne always loved going to the beach, but we used to go out to Pigeon Lake. You ever been there, Barbara? A few summers we even rented a cottage for part of the summer. Then the kids got bigger and began working in the summers and there didn't seem to be much point in going anymore."

Uncle Hal and Livvy are ambling back with their double-dipped cones dripping down onto their hands. "Mmmm. Yum," Livvy says, holding the cone in one hand and licking chocolate off the other.

"Barbara says she's starving," Auntie Sophie announces, "so we'll get everything ready and people can just eat whenever they want."

"That's okay," I say. "I guess I'm not as hungry as I thought I was."

Livvy gives me a look, but she doesn't say anything.

It is late afternoon by the time we get back into town. As soon as I can, I use the phone in the den to call Jim Beresford but a machine comes on saying the office won't be open until nine o'clock tomorrow morning.

"Whatcha doing?" Livvy bounces up and down in the doorway. "Uncle Hal is getting *The Wizard of Oz* for us to watch tonight."

"Big deal. We've seen it a hundred times." I think of Daddy sunk into the sofa, sipping his sherry, mouthing the words along with the characters. *I think we're not in Kansas anymore.*

"I want to see Toto." Livvy flounces off.

Somewhere there must be a telephone book. I pull open drawers and open doors in the wall unit, and finally find one in the drawer under the television. When I phone the hospital, the receptionist transfers me to a nurse at one of the nursing stations.

"Nursing Station 6C," a voice like an answering machine comes on. I wonder if I should talk to it. "What can I do for you?" it says.

I ask about Cosmo.

"Mr. Farber?" she says. "His condition is stable."

"What do you mean?"

"Are you a member of the family?" she asks.

"No. A friend."

"I see."

"Can I see him?"

"At the current time, visiting is restricted to family members and a few specified friends. What's your name?"

I tell her.

"I don't see it on the list."

"Honey," Auntie Sophie is smiling in the doorway, "you're welcome to use the phone just so long as you tell us who you're calling."

"Oh, I'm sorry," I say. "I couldn't get through anyway."

I wait until the dishwasher is making lots of noise after supper before I phone Nathan from the phone in the upstairs hall. Uncle Hal is getting the video ready in the den, with Livvy helping him.

"H-Hello." Between the dishwasher and whatever's going on at Nathan's house, I can barely hear him. "H-How are things g-going?"

"Okay. The Hetheringtons are okay. But I have a feeling something bad is happening with Cosmo."

"Is he still in the hospital?"

"He is, but only certain people can visit him. Family. Specified friends."

"Gee."

"I've got to get down there."

"Listen, pal, I'm good at these kinds of plans," Nathan says.

And I listen.

"We're just getting ready to start, honey," Auntie Sophie says when I go into the den. "Livvy's going to love this show. It was a favorite of Luanne and Laverne's. I wouldn't be surprised if they saw it three times."

I give Livvy the eyeball. She hasn't even told them she's seen it more times than Toto has hair on his little doggie chin.

"Can we have Rice Krispie squares?" Livvy refuses to look at me.

"You goose," Auntie Sophie laughs. "We've just got up from the supper table. Tell you what, though. When Dorothy gets to Shangri-La, then we'll get some munchies."

Emerald City, I want to say. Get your movies straight. But instead I smile at Sophie and Harold. "I've seen the movie a couple of times and I'm a bit tired so I think I'll go to bed early and read *Jane Eyre*. It'll probably put me to sleep in half an hour. Is that okay?"

"Is that okay!" Auntie Sophie jumps up from the sofa and grabs my hand.

"You sleep as much as you want to. You've had a pretty stressful time and your body is just telling you that you need extra sleep. It's the best thing, believe me."

"Goodnight, then." I squeeze Auntie Sophie's hand, smile at Uncle Hal.

"Goodnight, Barbara," he says through a blast of sound as he adjusts controls.

Livvy looks at me suspiciously for a minute but the MGM logo surfaces on the screen and she settles back into the sofa. "Oh, goodee," she says, trying to sound enthusiastic.

There are extra pillows in the closet in Luanne's room. I place them under the bedcovers and lump everything to make it look as much as possible like someone sleeping. I open

Jane Eyre and turn it over by the lamp. "Make sure the window is unlocked," Nathan told me on the phone. I do, and close the curtains.

Uncle Hal has given both Livvy and me a five-dollar allowance for the week. Livvy managed to spend hers in one swoop at the Seven-Eleven, but I have four dollars left. I check that it is still in my pocket, grab the survival bag and tiptoe up the stairs.

From down the hall, Dorothy is singing *Somewhere over the rainbow, bluebirds fly...*

It is two blocks to the bus stop, but Sunday service is not great in the suburbs. It is light enough to do word searches, and I am into my third one when the bus finally comes. Nathan has told me where to transfer downtown, and I wait again for the bus that will take me to the hospital.

I know my way around the emergency ward, and it is easy to slip past everyone and go down to the elevators. Things are quiet on the sixth floor. It looks like visitors are leaving. I wander down the hall, trying to see into the rooms without looking like some sort of a spy. An old woman in a wheelchair glares at me.

Finally, through one door, I see a figure in a

bed. He's all hooked up to hoses and his face is covered with an oxygen mask, but I see the nest of gold hair above his forehead. A woman sits beside his bed, holding his hand. She looks like a movie star, with white-gold hair and clothes that are shiny and silky.

"I'm Barbara Kobleimer, a friend of Cosmo's," I say to her. "Can I see him for a few minutes? He was my teacher at the clown workshop."

"Sure." She smiles at me, a tired smile. "I'm his sister, Annette. He may not be awake."

I stand by his bed. It's like the last time I saw Mama, but instead of Mama's thin face trying to smile, here is Cosmo's thin face with his eyes closed, so motionless I wonder if he is still breathing. But then there is a little shudder and his hand trembles.

"You can hold his hand," Annette says. "In fact, I think I'll slip out for ten minutes for a smoke so you have a little visit and I'll be right back. If he needs the nurse, just press this little buzzer here."

I take Cosmo's thin long hand in mine. It's stopped trembling and it feels cold, so I rub my palm back and forth over it to warm it. I don't know what to do, but it seems okay to talk to Cosmo even if he is sleeping.

"Would you believe it," I say. "I finally got to go back to Alberta Beach. Remember when we told about our most special time, and that was mine? Except it wasn't so special as it was before. I'm not sure why. The sun was shining and little kids were running in and out of the water, and there was even a pregnant lady in a bathing suit that made me think of Mama. But somehow it was all kind of a let-down. I tried to pretend it was really great because these people, the Hetheringtons, are trying like mad to make things good for Livvy and me. You would laugh at Livvy. She's sucking up to them and they feed her nonstop. I think she's happy, but she misses Daddy and Grandma. About once or twice a day she asks when we're going home. The funny thing is, I miss them, too. It's kind of silly, but I guess they needed me. The Hetheringtons, they're there for us, but we're not really there for them. Except, maybe Livvy. I think Livvy is more like they remember their daughters being when they were little. Harold—Uncle Hal—is goofy about model trains, and Livvy is real good at pretending she loves them, too. Auntie Sophie goes like a model train all day, cleaning and cooking and running errands. After supper she generally conks out on the sofa when we're watching TV."

I have been looking at Cosmo's hand all the time I've been talking, and now I look up past the tubes and blankets to his face, and his eyes are open. His gentle green eyes are fixed on my face. "Cosmo, you're going to get better. You have to get better. Livvy and I need you so badly." I feel a tremor along his fingers. "Oh, Cosmo," I say, and I can feel the tears starting at the edge of my own eyes, "you made everything different."

His sister has come back in. "Hey, Dreamboat, how are you doing?" she says.

But he closes his eyes again.

"We'd best not tire him," she says. "Thank you for coming."

"Goodbye, Cosmo," I say. "See you soon." At the door, I stop. It seems important to say something else. But what? There are no words.

Nathan is waiting for me in a chair by the nursing station.

"S-Sorry," he says. "Thought I could get here sooner but the old lady went kind of crazy."

I sit down beside him. For a minute I can't say anything.

"Are you o-k-kay?"

I find my voice. "He's so sick. I've never seen anyone so sick, since Mama. I'm afraid."

Nathan holds my hand as we make our way to the elevators and back through the emergency ward. "I'll ride the bus home with you," he says. "I don't really w-want to go home myself right now anyway. M-my mom said for me n-not to come home until I've grown up. Guess that means until I'm a few inches taller and have a six-pack in my hands."

"What started the fight?"

"Who knows. She's touchy as a h-hornet, because she and the b-boyfriend ran out of cigarettes and beer, and she knew I had cigarettes stashed somewhere but I wasn't saying where."

It's starting to get dark as the bus rambles through the crescents and drives of the south side. Nathan holds my hand and tells me about when his uncle died in the hospital a couple of years ago, his body hooked up to a tangle of tubes with plastic bags dripping fluids into him, and other bags taking fluids away.

"I know," I say. "It was like that with Mama

at the last. I only saw her once in the hospital. She didn't want me to come, I think."

Nathan walks me right to the house. The block is quiet. Everything is dark at the Hetheringtons. We move like shadows into the back yard where my bedroom window looks out onto one of Auntie Sophie's flowerbeds. Nathan pops the outer screen out of place like someone who has done it more than once. He smiles crookedly at me.

"You c-crawl in and I'll pop it back into place."

"Thanks, Nathan." I catch his hand, and suddenly he has his arms around me, and his face is against my cheek. Where do my hands go? I move them up and feel his long hair and then his lips brushing against mine.

"G-Good night," he says. "T-Try to call me tomorrow."

arly in the morning Livvy comes downstairs and crawls into bed with me.

"I had an accident," she says. She has managed to get into clean pajamas. Auntie Sophie has left extra underwear and nightclothes in her room.

"Are you okay?" I let her snuggle up to me.

"I want to go home."

"We can't just yet. Daddy isn't well."

"Maybe Uncle Hal could take us to see him and Grandma." She yawns and burrows into my back. We both fall back asleep.

It is Auntie Sophie who wakes us. "There you are, Livvy. It's time to get up, you two sleepyheads," she trills. "We've got a big day ahead. The dentist just after lunch for both of you, and Livvy, you have a doctor's appointment at 3:30, and I need to stop at the supermarket. I need whipping cream if I'm going to make Boston cream pie to go with the lamb chops for supper. Harold thought he might have time to go for me, but the hobby shop called with some pieces for that new line he's building, and when it comes to choosing between grocery shopping and that railway, well…I think we all know who wins out there. Oh, and Barbara, you need to get up right away because Mr. Beresford phoned and said he wanted to drop by and see you around 10:30. Said he wanted to take you out for coffee and, of course, I said I hope you don't mean real coffee, and he said…"

Jim Beresford.

I wait on the front doorstep for him.

"I want to go, too," Livvy says.

"Well, you can't."

"Baa!"

"Livvy, dear," Auntie Sophie calls through an open window. "You come and help me in the garden. We need a couple of new bouquets and you made such lovely ones the other day."

"Okay." She hops up and is gone.

I've started *A Tale of Two Cities*, one of the other novels Cosmo gave us the night we toted books from his place. *It was the best of times and the worst of times…*

Jim Beresford waves at me from the window of his car when he pulls up.

"Do you mind getting away for a few minutes?"

"No. I'd like to."

We drive to one of the coffee shops in Old Strathcona. Along the way he asks me how things are going at the Hetheringtons.

"Fine," I say.

"They let you go down to the hospital last night by yourself?"

"No." My face flushes with shame. "They didn't know I went."

"It's okay," he says, ordering a cappuccino for himself and hot chocolate for me. I remember Cosmo placing the same order at the Italian center. It seems like a long time ago.

"He meant a lot to you, didn't he? Mr. Farber."

"Cosmo."

"Cosmo."

"I phoned the hospital this morning," Jim Beresford says. He is looking at his coffee, not at me, as if there are cue cards in his cup for what he has to say. "He died quietly at three o'clock this morning. He'd been fighting AIDS, the doctor said, for over twelve years. He'd had pneumonia several times, but each time...You knew he had AIDS?"

I nod.

I don't want to cry in front of Jim Beresford, so I drink my hot chocolate in slow sips, and hear his quiet, caring voice going on.

Across the street, a sidewalk performer is doing a juggling act on the corner of Whyte and Fourth. He is dressed like a jack in a deck of cards, and the colored balls fly higher and higher. Then, magically, they return to nest in his hands. When he is finished, it seems to me that he bows to us where we sit at the coffee-shop window.

"Barbara?" Jim Beresford is asking me a question.

"There's a juggler out there."

"Seems to be a street festival going on all summer long in Old Scona."

Jim spoons up the last of the foam from his cappuccino cup. "So, do you want to give it some thought? About the memorial service, I mean?"

"Memorial service?"

"For Cosmo. I had a little chat with his sister. She's the one who told me you'd been up to see him last night. Actually, she phoned the department and got hold of me, said she'd gone back to Cosmo's apartment and your name was on a note attached to a box of books or something."

"Cosmo was giving all of his books that he had when he was a kid to Livvy and me. We were supposed to take them a few at a time, but we only had one chance."

"*A Tale of Two Cities?*" I didn't think he'd noticed my book when I got in the car.

"And *Jane Eyre*. Three or four other ones. Livvy makes me read *Winnie-the-Pooh* over and over again. Can Nathan come to the service, too?"

◆

On the day of the memorial service, Jim Beresford takes time off work to pick up Nathan and me and take us. Auntie Sophie has whisked Livvy away to a shopping mall to look at going-back-to-school clothes. There is a little part of me that thinks maybe Livvy should be coming, too, but then I think the memories she has of Cosmo have way more meaning to her than what people will be saying about him at the service. When I told her that Cosmo had died at the hospital, she went off by herself for awhile and wouldn't talk to anyone. Since then, she seems to ask questions about him and what happens when people die three or four times a day.

"Is he seeing Mama?"

"I don't know, Livvy." I seem to always be searching for words. "Some people think that when you die, your spirit stays around for awhile, sort of checking things out." I read this once in a magazine at the library. Some people who had been dead for a minute or two had risen above their bodies and had been able to watch everything that was going on. "Maybe Cosmo is watching us right now. I think he'd want us to remember the good times we had with him."

"Maybe he's remembering the bike accident."

"Maybe. Was that a good time? You did a lot of crying."

"I remember sherbet. That was a good time, wasn't it, Barbara?"

"Do you want me to go to the memorial service with you, honey?" Auntie Sophie asked. "Sometimes it just helps to have someone with you." I didn't want to hurt her feelings, but I definitely did not want Auntie Sophie sitting beside me. That's when I suggested it would be nice if she could get Livvy off somewhere for a couple of hours.

"Jim Beresford says he'll stay with me and drive me home after."

Nathan is waiting on his front step, smoking a cigarette. In the daylight, I see his yard is filled with stuff that looks like it wouldn't quite fit in the stucco townhouse. A freezer, a cabinet-TV with a cracked screen, an armchair. Nathan butts out his cigarette. He's wearing a white shirt and a bolo tie.

"H-How do you like the lawn ornaments?" he says, squeezing himself into the back seat of Jim Beresford's compact.

"Better than plastic pink flamingoes," Jim says, introducing himself. "You were in Cosmo's workshop, too? Did they end up canceling it?"

"N-No. Cosmo's friend J-Janice Jellicoe is doing it. She says call her J. J. She's supposed to be there today. At the service."

Jim Beresford and Nathan chat about the class as we drive to the Unitarian Church, but I catch Nathan's eye in the rear-view mirror. We have only talked on the phone a couple of times since Nathan took the bus home with me the night Cosmo died. I'm glad I'm wearing Mama's pink skirt and beads that I wore over to Cosmo's when Livvy and I visited him and he gave us gingerbread. They hadn't been in the box of things Jim Beresford brought with him the day he delivered Livvy to the Hetheringtons, so he visited Daddy at the treatment center and got the key. I went with him over to the house.

It was strange going into the house with no one there. Just the noise of the fridge running, but the television silent, and everything left just as if we'd all been suddenly sucked up into a spaceship by aliens.

Grandma's cigarette butts in her ashtray, a bone china cup and a teapot on her TV tray, an empty sherry bottle on the floor by the sofa, a half-eaten package of potato chips, some videos on the end table, *Titanic* on the top of the pile.

"These need to go back to the video store," I told Jim.

I made another box of my things and Livvy's from the upstairs bedrooms, taking down the photos from my room and tucking those on top.

"You look great, Barbara," Nathan whispers to me in the parking lot at the Unitarian Church. "Pretty skirt."

"It was Mama's," I say. "You look good, too. I like your tie."

"Uncle T-Ted's," Nathan grins.

The church is filled. I recognize some of the kids from the workshop.

Jessica-Marie in her lumberjack shirt and overalls. The boy with the ponytail is wearing a velvet vest embroidered with flowers and bees and butterflies. He and Nathan say, "Hey, man," to each other.

At Mama's funeral, I remember, a minister did just about all of the things there were to do, but here a lot of different people get up to talk.

"Th-That's J. J.," Nathan nudges me when a young woman with a tangle of red curls, a Barbra Streisand kind of nose and a wide friendly mouth takes her turn at the front. She smiles and nods at everyone, stops for a second and roots in her pockets for something, pulls out a red clown nose and puts it on. A titter ripples through the room.

"You might think this is for comic effect," she tells us, "but Cosmo, very aware of the Jimmy Durante protuberance midway between my eyes and my mouth, always said this was a cosmetic improvement for me. And, Cosmo, I do want to look as cosmetically perfect as possible for you today."

Cloud has slipped in late and sits beside us.

Her hair is strawberry-colored today, and she's wearing something that looks like a black cocktail dress along with logger's boots.

"Cosmo never thought of himself as a brave person," J. J. continues, "but, like many people living with AIDS, he had the courage to look at the future, to sense and prepare for closure. Most of you know that he lost his longtime companion, Roberto, five years ago, and I know he believed that what lay ahead was a step toward a reunion with the person he loved most in the world. He didn't talk about it as a possibility, but a certainty."

Across the aisle and a couple of rows down, I see Cosmo's sister. She is wearing a deep sea-green suit, her movie-star hair falling like Marilyn Monroe's to the collar. Cosmo's color—green. I can see only the side of her face, but the weariness from the hospital seems to be gone from it. She watches J. J. with a half-smile on her lips. An older woman sits beside her, cheeks moist with tears. Cosmo's mother?

"Cosmo and I used to talk about his funeral," J. J. is saying. "I guess he was always fascinated by the reasons people choose to get together. 'Yeah,' he would say in that terrible imitation of the Dead End Kids lingo that he would use when he was trying to make you laugh instead of cry. 'I tink a funereal ain't such a bad idea. People can get together and do a little remembering, a little eating, a little crying, listen to a little music, and—who knows—maybe a couple of people who don't even know each other might fall in love. Dat would be kinda nice, eh?'"

Nathan squeezes my hand.

"Cosmo was not a perfect person. You only had to listen to his Dead End Kids impression to know that, but God, he was pretty close to it." J.J. pauses and she bows her head for a moment, as if she is gathering her strength. "He had the gift that only certain special people have, an ability to change us in ways that we would never have thought possible."

As I watch J.J., I feel as if Cosmo is somewhere close by. I feel like a spotlight might suddenly come on and pick him out of the dark and he'll turn and look at all of us with a little look of surprise and a tip of the head. Maybe he will pluck a rose out of nowhere and he'll hold it out toward us. A gift.

Thank you, I want to say. I think of the cup of tea on the watermelon placemat on Cosmo's kitchen table. Thank you for the magic and the tea and being there for Livvy and me. Thank you for *Jane Eyre* and gingerbread.

Someone has taken J. J.'s place at the front of the auditorium. A young man with no hair, a shy smile, and a guitar. He begins to sing, so softly the words seem like something written on tissue paper. It is the song that the lady with the sad, gravelly voice sang on Cosmo's CD. *God Bless the Child.* As he sings, his voice gets louder and fills the church, but at the end, his voice falls again to a near whisper: *"God bless the child that's got his own. That's got his own."*

It is what Cosmo told us at the start of the clown workshop. Get your own. Make your own. Find something to hold onto.

◆

When the service is over, Jim and Nathan and I go to say hello to Cosmo's sister.

Annette introduces their mother to us. I notice a trace of Cosmo's grin in her wide smile. "It's nice to meet some of Cosmo's students," she says. "He worked with so many over the years."

"Barbara was a neighbor, too, I think," says Annette. "He left a box of stuff for you and your little sister. He had packages of things for about twenty different people in his closets, all labeled, with little notes. I thought you might be here today so I put your box of stuff in the trunk of my car."

"Do you want to open it now?" Jim Beresford says when he hefts the box out of her trunk. "Feels like it's filled with bricks."

"No, I think I'll wait." I want to be by myself when I open it.

There is only Uncle Hal at home when I am dropped back at the house.

"Why don't you give me a hand putting together this station house for my new line?" he calls out to me from across the basement, where he stands like a giant in the middle of a maze of miniature trains. "I could use some help."

"Sure," I say. "In a little while if that's okay. I've got just a little headache and I thought I might lie down for a half hour or so."

"Good idea. Nip it in the bud. You want an aspirin? I'm sure we've got aspirins around here somewhere."

"No, I'll be fine if I just close my eyes for a little."

I place Cosmo's box on the bed. There is an index card taped to the outside saying "For

Barbara and Olivia Kobleimer." When I pull the flaps open, there's a letter inside. It's what I was hoping there would be.

"Dear Barbara Stanwyck and Olivia de Havilland," Cosmo has scripted his note in green ink with a calligraphy pen. "I have put these books aside for you just in case we don't have enough visits to get them to your house a few at a time in grocery bags. It has been a delight getting to know the two of you. I feel you have become special friends, and that is why I feel especially comfortable leaving you the books. There is something about picking up a book and knowing that someone who has meant something to you has rested his fingers on each page, has savored the lines, thought about what the book has to say. I guess there is a kind of engagement of soul and spirit in the act of reading that maybe leaves the tiniest traces on the paper, like infinitesimal bits of stardust. So, know I am there, on these pages, reading along with you. Lots of love, Cosmo."

Savored. Engagement. Infinitesimal. The words are like exotic animals. I look at them again and again, pick up each of the books in turn, opening them, running my fingers along the endpapers, reading a line here and there. *A Traveller in Time. Treasure Island. The Sword in the Stone. David Copperfield. Wind in the Willows.* Some of the volumes are inscribed. *Love to Garson on his twelfth birthday—Aunt Charity. Merry Christmas Garson—Mommy and Daddy.*

CHAPTER SIXTEEN

S eptember is the best time, when summer holidays are over and school begins again. I am going to a large junior high school a few blocks from where the Hetheringtons live, and Livvy and I walk together to her elementary school on the way. Livvy dances along in her new back-to-school clothes. She knows that Auntie Sophie will be over to the school in a minute if she has an accident, but it's only happened once since school started.

The junior high is kind of scary, but it's easy to fade into the background when there are hundreds and hundreds of teenagers, and there are safe corners, like the library. At first I wasn't able to get into drama as an option, but Jim Beresford phoned the school counselor and my schedule was changed around. The drama teacher, Miss Eccles, has us doing a lot of improvising. Sometimes it seems as if Cosmo is at the back of the room watching, giving me hints about bits of business that will work. *Eat choco-*

lates that are soft and keep getting stuck to your fin-
gers. Think of the color red, let it bathe you, wash
inside you. Make little chirping noises, like a bird.
"You have a natural talent," Miss Eccles says. I
haven't told her what my middle name is.

The first time Livvy and I saw Daddy after he
got out of the treatment center, Jim Beresford
drove us to the house. Daddy met us at the door
and it seemed that in the weeks since we had
seen him he had shrunk, and the gray at the
edges of his hair had spread into the rest of it.

"I'll come back in an hour," Jim Beresford
said.

The living room looked strange with the
blinds open and sunlight showing all the raveled
corners of the furniture, the worn patches of carpet, the cigarette burns around Grandma's chair.
The TV sat silent, dead. Livvy sat still for about
one and a half minutes before she bounded off
to check all the parts of the house.

"I'm sorry," Daddy said when Livvy had gone
upstairs. I looked at him. The word seemed
strange coming from him, just as everything else
was strange. He looked down at his hands folded over his stomach. "It should have been better.
Your mama would have wanted it better."

I wandered across the room and stared out the window. Crispy Dan's panel truck was parked in front of the Perths with a flat tire, giving it a sad, drunken look.

"It will be better." Daddy's voice was soft, the kind of voice you use in a library. "In awhile you'll be able to come back. I just have to..."

"Hey," Livvy shouted from the top of the stairs, "guess what!"

"What?" Daddy said.

"I found my Pocahontas coloring book." She pounded downstairs and bounced like Tigger into the living room. "I'm going to stay here now so I can color."

"You leave it here," Daddy said, his voice a little stronger, "and you can color in it whenever you come over."

"But I want to stay. I don't want to go." Livvy folded her arms and turned her back on us. "Where's Grandma?"

"She's in the hospital for awhile." Daddy tried to force a cheerfulness to his voice. "She'll be home before too long."

"I want her home now." Livvy began to cry and she was still weeping when Jim Beresford came to pick us up.

"It's okay," Daddy said. "You take the coloring book with you."

◆

Since Daddy came over to the Hetheringtons for my birthday supper a week ago, Livvy has convinced herself that it is only a matter of time until he can come and live here, too.

Daddy was very quiet all through the supper, complimenting Auntie Sophie on her roast ham and scalloped potatoes, the birthday cake covered with icing-sugar flowers.

"Just one of my little hobbies." Auntie Sophie seemed reluctant to spoil the perfection of the top of the cake by lighting the fourteen twirly pink candles. "Cake decorating."

"Hardly just a hobby," Uncle Harold beamed at us. "Sophie's won prizes. What was that last trophy for?"

A little spark came into Daddy's eye when I opened my gift from him, a video copy of *The Lady Eve* starring Henry Fonda and Barbara Stanwyck.

"Now there's a cake decorating scene in this movie that'll leave you rolling on the floor. I thought your mama was going to choke, she laughed so hard. We went to see it two nights in a row when they did that Henry Fonda retrospective at the Varscona."

"I want to see it," Livvy announced, her mouth full of cake. "Daddy, you can stay and watch it."

But he couldn't. And the next day, Jim Beresford dropped by to see me after school and told me Daddy was drinking again, by himself at the house, shored up with bottles of sherry and piles of videos.

Grandma Kobleimer is still in the nursing home. At the end of August, she stumbled and fell and broke her hip. The Hetheringtons took Livvy and me to see her when she got out of the hospital and back into the home, but she kept going to sleep so we didn't stay very long. Since then, we have been back to see her once, but she didn't recognize Livvy or me. "Mildred." She grabbed my sleeve. "I don't want you seeing him anymore. There's going to be nothing but trouble." We didn't stay long that time, either.

Nathan is going to a junior high in the west end. He hates the school and has been missing a lot of classes. Drama and music are the only subjects he likes. The Hetheringtons let Livvy and me go to the downtown library on Saturdays, and Nathan meets us there. Sometimes we go across the street into the theater with its little indoor park and waterfall. Livvy likes to hop around the trails through the shrubbery and flowers, and it gives Nathan and me a minute to sit together. When he is really down about how things are going at school and at home, I try to think of what Cosmo might say.

"Yeah, Mary S-Sunshine," he says. "I know. Go see my counselor. Tell him I need a different family. T-Tell him to make my life good."

"No," I say. "You're the only one who can make your life good. Cosmo said…"

"Cosmo, Cosmo, Cosmo…"

"Cosmo said we need to fight sometimes when the people around us are harming us. He said…"

"Yeah, if I say that to my m-mom, she'll smack me across the room, and her b-boyfriend'll crack a rib or two for good measure."

"Sometimes we get hurt getting into the lifeboats," I say.

Nathan shakes his head, but he's smiling.

"Hey, look at me," Livvy calls from a catwalk far above us. She's on top of the world.